KAZAAM™

A novelization by Nicholas Edwards
From the screenplay by Christian Ford and Roger Soffer
And story by Paul M. Glaser

SCHOLASTIC INC.
New York Toronto London Auckland Sydney

ISBN 0-590-93104-0

12 11 10 9 8 7 6 5 4 3   6 7 8 9/9 0 1/0

Printed in the U.S.A.   40

First Scholastic printing, July 1996

1

Max Connor was supposed to be in his social studies class, but he was in no hurry. He *enjoyed* missing class. The halls at Crocker Junior High School were completely empty, and it was very peaceful. He strolled down the dingy hallway, kicking at chipped linoleum with untied high-tops.

There were footsteps behind him, and he turned just in time to see a patroling hall monitor. Quickly, Max ducked around the corner and out of the way. He had gotten detention so many times lately that he couldn't even remember what it was like to have a free afternoon. He held his breath, and the hall monitor didn't even notice him.

Max grinned, and pushed away from a row of lockers. If he was lucky, maybe it would only take him another — oh, say, ten minutes — to make it to class.

Suddenly, a hand grabbed the collar of his flannel shirt and yanked him backward into the boys' bathroom. The tile walls were covered with graffiti, and most of the stall doors had been broken for years. Max found himself lying on the grimy floor, staring up at three of the meanest kids in the whole school. In fact, they were probably the meanest kids in the whole *town!*

The leader of the gang was Elito, who was always so hyper that he actually *twitched.* His two sidekicks were named Z-Dog and Carlos. Z-Dog was very small for his age and he never stopped laughing and making fun of people. Carlos, on the other hand, was so tall and skinny that he looked like a teenage scarecrow.

Elito smiled cruelly at Max. Then he whipped out a can of black spray paint and shook it up. He carefully sprayed around Max's body, making an outline like that around a corpse on the floor.

Max never liked to show that he was scared, so he put on a cocky grin. "Don't tell me this is about lunch money again," he said.

Instead of smiling back, Elito snapped open a sharp butterfly knife.

Max gulped. It looked like he was in *big* trouble now!

"It's a math problem," Elito said in his hoarse voice. "If we took all the dough from a dork on the floor — would it be enough?"

With that, Elito and his friends ripped through Max's pockets, searching for money. Carlos sneered when he found a packet of chalk in Max's vest pocket and threw it on the floor. Then he reached deeper into the pocket and came out with a handful of change.

Z-Dog leaned over to count the money. "Whoa, two dollars and seventy cents," he snickered. "We're gonna be living large with this, boys."

Elito and Carlos both scowled. They had obviously expected to find a lot more money. This wouldn't even be enough to buy them each a slice of pizza after school.

Elito snatched at a small pair of dice hanging around Max's neck. "These worth something?" he asked.

Even though Max was still pinned to the floor, he grabbed the dice back. "It's nothing," he said nervously. "Belonged to my dad." Somehow, he had to think of a way to get rid of these three punks before he got hurt. "Look, if you want a real score —" Then, he stopped, as though he had blurted out a secret.

Elito and his friends leaned closer, their eyes narrowing.

"Yeah?" Carlos asked, and held up his clenched fist.

Max stared at each of them in turn, trying to think of something smart to say. "I nabbed a locker key," he answered finally. "A *serious* key. But I can't get close. Everyone there knows me."

Now the junior gangsters were intrigued.

"Everyone *where* knows you?" Carlos asked.

Max shook his head. "Uh-uh," he said. "You want in, we make a deal. Seventy–thirty."

Z-Dog's mouth dropped open. "Seventy–thirty?! Thirty–*seventy*, dorkhead."

Max sat up, rejecting that idea with an abrupt wave of his hand. "Bogus," he said. "Sixty–forty is my last offer."

Fed up, Elito put his boot on Max's chest and pushed him back down. "Shut up!" he ordered. "It's fifty–fifty — *if* the key's any good."

Max glared right back at him, determined to be just as tough. "It's the Wholesale Mart," he improvised off the top of his head. "Fifth and Broadway. Rolexes, gold chains, who knows what else. Third aisle. Locker eight-eight-two. Upstairs. And all you need is . . ." He paused, and opened his right hand to show them a precious key.

There was a long minute of silence. Then Elito grabbed the key away from him.

"We'll, uh, be in touch," Elito said, and winked at him. Then he lifted his boot from Max's chest and motioned for his friends to follow him.

The gang noisily left the bathroom, Z-Dog cackling all the way. Max held his breath as he watched them go. Once the door had swung shut, he shivered and slumped back down into his spray-painted outline.

That one had been too close for comfort! And what was going to happen when Elito and the oth-

4

ers realized that he had lied about the key? He didn't really want to find out.

After a few minutes, Max let out his breath and sat up. It really was time to go back to class. He ran some water in the sink, and splashed it over his face. His hair looked all spiky from the water, and he tried to pat it down. Then he picked up the dented box of chalk, and slogged down the hall to his classroom.

His teacher, Mrs. Duke, looked at her watch. Then she frowned and put her hands on her hips. "Another alien abduction, Max?" she asked.

He handed her the battered chalk she had sent him to get in the first place.

"They wanted my optic lobes," he explained, "but they didn't get a thing...."

"Very funny," Mrs. Duke said without smiling.

"I aim to please, ma'am," Max agreed. He turned to find his desk — and walked right into a chair!

The whole class laughed, but Mrs. Duke was not amused. Impatiently, she held out her empty hand.

"You forgot something. I need the key to the supply closet, Maxwell," she said.

He gave her his most innocent shrug. "What key?"

"To the supply closet," she said, gritting her teeth.

"I-I left it in the door, Mrs. Duke," he stammered.

Mrs. Duke did not like that answer. *At all.* "And you *also* left us without enough time to hear your presentation," she reminded him.

Max hung his head and tried to look sorry. The truth was that he hadn't even *prepared* a presentation. Just then, the bell rang, and he thought he was safe.

"But I want to hear it anyway," Mrs. Duke decided. "Right here. After school."

Max sighed, as the rest of the class laughed at him. Now he had detention.

Again.

2

Late that afternoon, he finally straggled home from school. He and his mother lived in an old, weathered apartment building that had seen better days. They didn't have much money, but his mother worked very hard and she always paid the rent on time.

When he got inside, he saw his mother, Alice, in the living room. She was wearing a frilly apron over her factory uniform, and she looked tired. Of course, she almost always looked tired when she got home from work. There was an old vacuum cleaner on the floor, and she was trying to fix it with a box of tools.

Alice waved at him with the large wrench in her hand. "Don't tell me," she said. "You were kidnapped by gypsies and sold to the circus."

Max just shrugged as he dropped his knapsack on the floor. "Can I help it if Mrs. Duke is a very angry man trapped in a woman's body?" he asked.

His mother nodded wisely. "Ah," she said. "Another homework malfunction. And gosh, what a surprise. Detention. *Again*."

Max grinned sheepishly.

"The only good thing," his mother went on, "is that you weren't here when we were . . . *robbed*."

She held up the vacuum cleaner — which had no motor inside.

Since he had been caught in the act, Max decided to deny everything. "What kind of maniac would steal the motor out of your Hoover?" he asked sweetly.

Alice didn't buy that for a minute. But she decided to change the subject, anyway. "You were supposed to come home and help me clean up the apartment today," she said. "Remember?"

The place *was* kind of a mess. And yes, Max had forgotten. Besides, what was the big deal? Travis had been her boyfriend for a long time, and he came over for dinner a lot. "It's just *Travis*, Mom," he said.

"And just what's that supposed to mean?" she wanted to know.

"You told me — men are like buses," he answered. "There's always another one."

Alice looked indignant. "I never said that!" Then she saw that Max was laughing. She relaxed and shoved a dust cloth into his hand. "Look, Travis spends all day working hard," she said. "The least we can do is make our home look nice for him."

"Why?" Max asked. "It's not like he lives here."

His mother's expression stiffened a little, but he wasn't sure why. Before he could ask, she had pushed him in front of the mirror.

"What's this?" she asked, pointing to his rumpled hair. "A dreadlock?" Then she touched one of his cowlicks. "Look, a tiny living creature!"

Max squinted at the mirror. As far as he was concerned, his hair looked perfectly normal.

Alice took out a comb to straighten the tangled mess. Then she pointed at his sixth-grade school picture from the year before. In it, Max looked clean and tidy.

"Honey, try and look like this guy," she suggested.

Max liked his hair just fine, but he picked up the comb and got to work.

His mother watched him. There was something she seemed to want to tell him, but she didn't say anything. And before she could even try, the front door flew open.

It was Travis, home from work. He was a firefighter, and he was still wearing his blue uniform.

"Hey, guys. Looking good, Max," he said cheerfully. Then he dropped his jacket on the only clean chair and gave Alice a quick kiss. "And you're not so bad, yourself."

Alice smiled back at him. "Thanks, mister."

Travis carried a bag of Chinese takeout over to the dining room table. He also had rented a video, and he tossed it over to Max.

"Max, ever heard of Buster Keaton?" he asked.

Max frowned at the unfamiliar movie title. "Isn't he some dead black-and-white guy?"

"Yeah," Travis admitted. "But he's a *funny* dead guy." He turned to Alice. "You, uh, tell him . . . ?"

Max looked up sharply, just in time to see his mother flinch. "Tell me what?" he asked suspiciously.

Alice hesitated.

Now he was *really* suspicious. "Tell me *what*?" Max repeated himself.

"Max," Alice started, her voice very gentle. "Travis and I — want to get engaged."

Max was caught off guard by that, and his eyes widened.

"B-but I thought he was just coming over for dinner," he stuttered.

"We wanted to wait until all of the papers were signed," Alice said.

Max gave her a confused look. "Papers? What papers?"

"The divorce papers," she explained. "There were some things left unsigned, by your — father."

Max blinked. "My father?" Then he blinked again. "You said you didn't know where he was."

Alice looked away to avoid his accusing expression. "I didn't," she said, but she didn't sound very convincing.

Seeming uncomfortable and wanting to help, Travis stepped forward. "Look," he said, putting

10

his hand on Max's shoulder. "What matters is that now you, and your mom, can move on with your lives. That's why we want to get engaged."

Max ignored him. "What about me?" he asked his mother. "Why didn't you ask me?"

Alice sighed. "Max —" she began.

"Why didn't you ask *me!*" he shouted. How could she *do* this to him? He threw the video on the floor as hard as he could and then ran out of the apartment.

Once he was outside, Max tore down the street on his BMX bike. He was so angry that he purposely slammed into every trash can he could find and knocked them over. In fact, he was so upset that he didn't even notice that Elito, Carlos, and Z-Dog were following him.

Max pedaled up one street, and down another. As he wheeled around one corner, a pickup truck screeched to a halt in front of him. Max stopped short, so startled that he forgot how upset he was.

As he turned around to go the other way, a group of high school gang members surrounded him. They were all scowling and holding bicycle chains.

Vasquez, the sneering dark-haired leader of the gang, swaggered over to him. He was brandishing a baseball bat and looked very dangerous. He was also Elito's bigger, meaner brother.

"Understand you're messing with my little brother," he growled.

Max swallowed hard. "Wait a minute, don't tell me," he said, his voice shaking a little. "They couldn't get the key in the lock."

Elito stepped out from behind Vasquez. His arms were folded across his chest, and his face was twisted in an ugly scowl.

"There *were* no lockers, Maxy," he said with an angry smile.

"And your map was a joke!" Z-Dog chimed in.

"I'm not happy, Max," Vasquez added, as he swung his baseball bat back and forth. "I'm not happy at all."

Max stared at them, his heart racing with fear. If he was going to escape, he had to move fast! He quickly aimed his bike up the bumper of the pickup truck and spun around on the hood. Before the gang had time to react, he was already pedaling away.

"After him!" Vasquez yelled.

Quickly, the gang piled into the truck.

Max barreled down the sidewalk on his bicycle, dodging past street lamps and telephone poles. The truck sped after him, with the gang members yelling threats the whole way.

Not sure what else to do, Max cut into a vacant lot. The truck swerved right after him. There was a half-demolished building up ahead, and Max rode toward it. The upper floors were in ruins, but maybe he could hide downstairs.

There was a sign in front of the building that

said DANGER: KEEP OUT! Max leaned all of his weight to one side. He dropped his bike, slid under the yellow tape that blocked off the building, and ran inside.

He careened down a crumbling hallway. The gang leaped out of the truck and came charging after him. Hearing their pounding footsteps, Max ran as fast as he could.

He tore up the splintered stairs to the third floor. But suddenly, the rotten boards crumbled under his feet, and the floor collapsed beneath him.

He was falling!

3

Max plunged through the second- and first-
story floors in a waterfall of sawdust. Finally, he landed in the basement in a heap of old
papers and filth. The garbage smelled horrible,
but at least it had broken his fall.

For a second, he was too stunned to move. Then
he heard the gang's footsteps overhead. Why
couldn't they just give up and leave him alone?

Max burrowed deeper into the disgusting trash,
and his head bumped into an oversized boom box.
He must have hit the power button, because it ac-
cidentally flicked on. Lights began flashing on the
boom box.

To his complete surprise, smoke began to billow
out of the worthless old, duct-taped wreck.

Then he heard a syncopated thumping sound,
like forty electric bass guitars playing at once. It
was so loud that he knew the gang would find him
any second!

Max tried to turn off the boom box with frantic

fingers. The machine's lights only glowed more brightly. The thumping became music, and there seemed to be some kind of screaming words in another language, too.

Suddenly, Vasquez used both hands to rip Max out of the trash heap. Max fought to get free, but it didn't work. His scrambling foot hit the eject button on the boom box. The cassette window slowly yawned open, and released a puff of dust into the air.

"You little jerk!" Vasquez yelled at him. "You think you got *skills*?"

Max opened his mouth to answer, but nothing came out.

The outraged gang surrounded him. They were all scowling, and their fists were clenched.

From within the trash heap, the ominous beat continued to swell. The unintelligible words were starting to take form, but they still didn't make any sense.

"— *inshallah bismillah nur al-dee, inshallah bismillah nur al-dee* —" the boom box seemed to be chanting.

Max did his best to smile at Vasquez and the rest of the gang. "Uh, guys," he said. "Why don't we just pretend this never happened?"

The gang just moved closer to him.

Then the entire mound of debris erupted into a cyclone of trash. Max and the gang were knocked to the floor by the force of the explosion. They all tried to duck as they were pelted by a blinding flurry of garbage.

The spinning tornado quickly became a form. It seemed to be the shape of a man in an ancient robe. Then a spinning turban appeared at the top of the form. A single, dented soda can twirled wildly until a size 22 sandal crushed it into an aluminum pancake.

The music was thumping more loudly. Max was amazed when he realized that it sounded just like rap.

"Who dare to wake me!" a deep male voice shouted.

Max and the gang stared up at the huge figure in horror. The man glared down at them, wearing a decrepit robe with a dirty, jeweled buckle. He was impossibly tall, imposingly powerful, and incredibly mad. He looked like some kind of insane genie.

The man went on with his Arabic-flavored groove. *"Ain't gonna make this a mystery,"* he rapped. *"Don't wanna do time on your wishes three!"*

Just then, Vasquez went for his switchblade. With one lightning-quick move, the man knocked it away.

"Watch it boy, you don't wanna dis me," he said, still rapping in his Baghdad beat. *"Or I'll dish out my misery!"*

Elito stepped forward with his bicycle chain.

The big man flicked the swinging chain away

with one finger. Then he raised himself to his full awesome height.

They all, including Max, gasped and backed away.

"Now who's that sorry wanna-be, that — disturbed — my — ZZZs!" the genie-like man roared.

Everyone in the gang pointed at Max. Then they fled up the stairs in a complete panic.

The giant's eyes settled on the last person left in the basement — Max. He leaned closer to focus on this insect.

Max turned away, praying for three seconds to escape. But then the man leaped in front of him and blocked the stairs.

"If you wanna be number one, I'm sorry, boy, that's been done," the man rapped. *"But if you got da itches, for a sack of riches, don't matter how avaricious! I'm the man to grant your wishes!"*

Max tried to run anyway, but he bounced right off the big man like a pinball. He picked himself up and darted around the gigantic man.

"Hey, don't turn your back on me!" the big guy said, and he slid over to block the exit. Then he raised his arms for the grand finale of his rap. *"I'm a man of the ages, straight outta the pages (hang on, I'm contagious)."* He turned to one side and sneezed theatrically. Then he resumed his rap. *"I'm outrageous, spontaneous, you can't contain this, I am . . . KA-ZAAM!"*

Kazaam. That must be the giant's name.

17

The giant finished his rap with a flourish and waited for applause. But nothing happened. Kazaam looked confused, and repeated the supernatural flourish. There was still no applause.

"I, uh, I'm really happy for you," Max said finally.

There was a brief silence, and they looked at each other. Then Max bolted up the steps.

"Hey, where do you think you're going?!" Kazaam called after him. "Make your three wishes, and I'm outta your face. So I'm back in my box, and outta this place!"

Safe at the top of the stairs, Max looked down at Kazaam.

"Excuse me, mister very-tall-psychopathic-dork-in-the-basement," he said politely. "I don't think you're ordering anybody."

The big guy put his huge hands indignantly on his hips. "Don't you realize who I am?" he asked. "I'm your genie!"

Max couldn't hold off a tiny smirk. "In that case," he said, and pretended to think for a minute, "I wish I was as big as you, only not so stupid!"

With that, he turned and ran.

Kazaam stared after him, stunned. "That's not a wish," he bellowed. "That's an insult!"

Max just kept running.

4

Max found his damaged BMX bike up on the first floor. He grabbed it and tried to pedal outside. The wheels were bent, and forcing them to turn was hard work. Finally, he made it out of the building and rode underneath the rope with the DANGER sign on it.

"Besides," a voice next to him said conversationally, "I don't do those kind of wishes."

Max was startled to see that Kazaam had somehow escaped from the basement and beaten him outside. It was even more strange to see the giant man smiling kindly at him, instead of looking scary.

"I do *material* wishes, see?" Kazaam explained. "Stuff. Things."

Whoever this guy was, he was *weird*. But Max just nodded pleasantly at him and kept going.

Kazaam looked very perplexed. "You gotta want *something*, kid!"

"You want to pull the wool over someone's eyes,

get a sheep," Max advised. Then he ducked through the broken fence, dragging his bike along behind him.

It was dusk, and Max kept to the shadows. He didn't see the gang around, but they might be hiding. He had already had enough narrow escapes for one day!

Back at the building, Kazaam sighed deeply. This kid was pretty tough. But he went after Max, bounding along right next to him.

"Oh, no," Max groaned. "You again."

"It's only 'cause this world really *really* gives me tension, that I'm gonna do something I don't ordinarily do," Kazaam told him. "One time, and one time only. I'm gonna beg. *Please*, make a wish."

The gang really did seem to be gone, so Max stopped walking. Maybe the best way to get rid of this guy was to play along.

"All right," Max said. "Give me a car. Jaguar. Black XKE."

"Car? Jaguar? Black XKE? *Okay!*" Kazaam answered, his expression very relieved. "Now you're talking. A Jaguar. Black. Better stand back."

Kazaam cracked his knuckles and shook the kinks out of his neck. Then he took a deep breath and fired out his special incantation.

"*I am . . . Kazaam!*" he shouted, and threw the magic out with both hands.

Nothing happened. Nothing at all.

"Okay, great try," Max said. "Keep in touch, will ya?" He shook his head, and pedaled his crooked bike down the street.

Kazaam was dumbfounded by his magical misfire. His powers *always* worked! He closed his eyes and gathered all of his strength.

"I got this Jaguar," he mumbled. "Black." He waved his arms. "And I am . . . Kazaam!"

His magic malfunctioned again, and he disappeared in a bright explosion of sparks.

Max, who was trudging along up ahead, didn't even notice. He was riding through a vacant lot when he came face-to-face with Vasquez and the gang. Max instantly reversed direction so he could get away.

The boys moved to block his way, and he was surrounded again.

"Hey!" Max called over his shoulder nervously. "Big guy! Kazoo!"

But Kazaam was gone, leaving only a small wisp of smoke and a few stray sparks behind.

An evil smile spread across Vasquez's face. "Nighty-night, little boy," he said.

Then the whole gang jumped on him!

It was much later when Max finally made it home. He eased the front door of the apartment open and peered inside. Lights were on in the kitchen, and he could hear Alice and Travis talking seriously. Max limped toward his room, carrying what was left of his bike.

Max heard his mother come hurriedly out to the hall. When she flicked on the overhead light, she gasped. Max's face was badly bruised and scratched, and his clothes were ripped, too.

"Max, are you all right?" she asked in a worried voice. "What happened, honey?"

"Nothing," he muttered.

"But — look at your face," his mother said, sounding as though she were close to tears. "Come out to the kitchen and I'll get you cleaned up."

Travis had followed her out to the hall to see what was going on.

"Hey," he said, also looking concerned. "Did you get in a fight, Max?"

"I'm okay, okay?" Max snapped. "Just leave me alone." He went into his room and slammed the door. He had just flung himself facedown on his bed when he heard someone enter the room.

Max turned from his bed and glared at Travis. "I said I wanted to be alone!"

Travis ignored that, coming all the way into the room. He stopped when he spotted a scorched, hand-built contraption of tailpipes and fly valves.

"Don't touch that," Max warned him.

Travis grinned at him. "You're not building a neutron bomb, are you?" he asked jovially. "That could be a little dangerous."

Max didn't smile back.

There was an awkward silence, and then Travis tried again.

"Are you okay?" he asked, sitting on the edge of Max's desk. "You want to tell me what happened?"

Max wouldn't even look at him.

Travis sighed. "You don't like me very much, do you," he said.

Max didn't respond.

"Max," Travis started. He stopped, trying to find the right words. "I know I can never take the place of your father. And I don't intend to. I really love your mom, and I want to marry her."

Max still didn't say anything.

"But this isn't just about me and your mother," Travis went on. "This is about you, too. I know that." He paused. "Look, Max, I'd like for us to be friends."

Max turned away completely.

"Well, okay," Travis said. He sighed and got up. "Any time you want to talk . . ."

Max still didn't answer, and Travis left the room. Once the door had closed, Max turned on his stereo. He cranked the volume up as high as it would go. Then he fell back onto his bed and stared up at the ceiling.

Years before, he had pasted a thousand stick-on stars above his bed. They glowed on the ceiling in wild constellations. It was a whole universe, built by Max. He looked at his stars for a while, and then closed his eyes. He could hardly wait to fall asleep and forget that this day had ever happened.

Up above him, one of the homemade stars magically turned into a shooting star. It flashed brilliantly across the ceiling, and then crashed silently into the wall in a wave of sparks.

5

In the morning, sunlight flooded through his window and woke up Max. He yawned and rolled out of bed. He was stiff and achy from the fight, but felt okay otherwise.

The apartment was very quiet. Usually, he could hear the radio playing or the morning news on the television. He wandered out to the kitchen, but his mother didn't seem to be home.

"Mom?" he called.

There was no answer, but he saw a note on the refrigerator. It said: *Had to cover Brenda's shift. Back for dinner. Do your homework. XOXO — Mom.*

Max sighed, and crumpled up the note. It was really too bad that his mother had to work so hard. He grabbed a hard-boiled egg and a jar of peanut butter from the refrigerator. Then he carried them out to the dining room. His schoolbooks and a lot of his mother's bills and papers were on the table, but he shoved them aside.

He was just biting into the egg when he saw a formal divorce decree on top of the papers. The man's name on the form was his father's, Nicholas Matteo. Max pulled the sheet over to look at it more closely, and the piece of egg fell right out of his mouth.

The address listed for his father was right downtown in the city where they lived! In fact, it was only a couple of miles away!

For years, his mother had told him that she didn't know where his father was, or how to get in touch with him. Could he really have been living right here in town all this time? How could she lie to him like that?

Max left the apartment, forgetting all about breakfast. He headed straight for the downtown district. It was rush hour and the streets were very crowded. He marched purposefully down the sidewalk, passing industrial and commercial buildings. He paused every so often to check the numbers on the buildings, and figure out where he was.

He had just stopped at a crosswalk and was waiting for the light to change when he saw something move out of the corner of his eye. It was Kazaam, foolishly trying to hide his bulk behind a skinny light pole.

Max scowled and ran across the street. Why wouldn't this joker just leave him alone? What did he have to do to get the guy to take the hint? Max ducked down an alley, hoping to elude him. But he only made it a few yards before he saw that Kazaam had gotten ahead of him again.

The big man looked very silly, as he tried to camouflage himself behind a tabloid newspaper. Much shorter pedestrians were crossing in front of him, and he tried to hide behind them, too.

Max whirled around to go back the other way. To his surprise, he walked right into Kazaam's broad leg. Max stopped and stared up at him incredulously. How did this guy move so fast, anyway?

"Hi," Kazaam said, and gave him an affable grin. "Don't you *wish* you had an ice-cream cone?" He whipped a double-dip chocolate-chip ice-cream cone out from behind his back. The only problem was that it was upside down.

Max looked at the giant with great pity. "Are you like, really lonely, or something?" he asked.

Kazaam frowned, and thought that over for a minute. Then he looked down to see the melting ice cream running through his fingers. It dripped onto the sidewalk and then fell off the cone completely.

Max just shook his head and kept walking. Kazaam followed him, and Max did his best to ignore his huge shadow.

Up ahead, there was a three-story music club called the Music Boxx. Max looked up and realized that it was the same address he had read on the divorce papers.

The building had once been a stately bank, but it had been rebuilt. Now the outside walls were punched through with steel beams and strapped with mammoth chains. It was as though construction debris had risen up to form a larger-than-life music box, right in the middle of the inner city.

Kazaam was impressed. "Wow," he said. "You live here?"

Max looked up at the massive club, feeling a little awed. His *father* must live here. "Yeah," he responded, trying to hide his uncertainty. "I built it, too."

"*Cool*," Kazaam said.

Max stood up on his toes to peer through one of the dusty windows. Where was the door to this place, anyway?

"So, anyway," Kazaam went on. "I still owe you one. In fact, I owe you *three*."

"Yeah, right," Max said sarcastically. "Your wishes are just so spectacular, I don't think I could bear another right now." He turned and walked down the alley to look for an entrance.

Kazaam followed him. "Uh, look, before. Last night, I mean, when you made your first wish. That kind of thing can happen to any genie. I was just a little rusty."

Max turned the corner just as a sleek Mercedes limo came gliding out of the building.

"Yo, Max!" Kazaam yelled to warn him.

Max jumped out of the way, and the limo cruised

by. The back window was open and his eyes locked on a powerful-looking man eating a plate of jumbo shrimp. They stared at each other. Max was transfixed by the man's ice-blue eyes. Then the window rolled up smoothly and the man's eyes disappeared behind the smoked glass.

Kazaam snapped his fingers. "Hey, I've got it! Want one of *those* cars, instead of the Jaguar?"

Max shook his head. "I don't know, man. They must really miss you back at the nice building with the padded walls," he said.

There was a door in front of him, and he pulled on the handle. It opened, and he went inside the club. The atmosphere was like a different world of glamour and celebrity. The ceilings were high, the furnishings were plush, and the whole place reeked of money and success. A work crew was up front, prepping for another long night of hot music and capacity crowds.

Max couldn't help gawking at the funky room. A very tall man walked by carrying a large anvil case and Max reached out to stop him.

"Excuse me, sir," he said. "I'd like to find Mr. Matteo?"

The man lowered the case, and Max saw that it was Kazaam.

"Make a wish, I'd be happy to tell you," Kazaam answered with a wide grin.

Max shook his head. What did he have to *do* to get this guy to go away and leave him alone?

There was a windowed office high above the floor, and Max headed for the stairs. He saw a long hallway with impressive mahogany doors. Each of the doors had a gold nameplate and Max squinted to read them. One of them must have his father's name on it.

A receptionist was sitting at the front desk, but he snuck past her and down the hall.

"Hey, Nick!" a woman inside one of the offices was saying. "This guy here says no to the mobile unit permits."

Max crept forward to peer into the office. Two men and a woman were all talking on separate telephones. There was a big show tonight, and they had lots of work to do to get ready.

The woman held her telephone out to the bigger man. He was wearing an expensive, three-piece suit, had a Rolex on his wrist, and his hair was neatly slicked back. In fact, he was the perfect image of a flashy and successful businessman. What was more important was that the woman had called him *Nick*. Nick was his father's name.

"Who am I talking to?" the man asked the woman before he took the phone.

"Paul Shea," she told him. The woman was kind of pretty and she had on a tight sweater and an extremely short miniskirt.

Nick nodded, and picked up the receiver. "Mr. Shea, this is Nick, the manager," he said in a hearty voice. "But not for long, unless you give me a hand, know what I mean? I'm going to have some *very* popular musicians asking why the newest club in town can't hack a live recording, know what I'm saying?" He paused to listen briefly. "Okay. What I'm *saying* is, I'm going to have the best table in the house, set aside especially for *you*." He listened again, and broke into a smile. "Yeah? Okay, then, Paul, buddy. See ya tonight."

As he hung up, the receptionist came over with a tray of sandwiches. Nick picked one up and took a bite. He made a face and dropped the sandwich back on the tray.

"Cindi, I love you," he said, "but if I wanted *pressed* turkey, I'd have run it over myself."

Cindi quickly left the room, probably to get some fresh sandwiches. As she opened the door, Max was exposed, waiting out in the hall.

For the first time in his life, there was nothing standing between him and his father. It was a moment he had been waiting for *forever*. He stepped forward, with his heart beating wildly.

"Who are you?" Nick demanded.

Max took a deep breath. This was the man he had always wanted to know. This was his *father*. "I'm . . . Max," he said.

6

After introducing himself, Max waited for his father's reaction. He was expecting a big hug, but a wide smile and "Wow! How great to see you, son!" would do. At the very least, he expected to get a "Hello."

Instead, Nick turned to his assistant, Theo. "Theo, you call a messenger or something?" He waved Max away. "Try downstairs, kid."

Max stared at him, his mouth agape. What was going on? Okay, it had been a long time, but shouldn't his father *recognize* his own son?!

Nick started down the hall without even glancing at him again. But when he noticed Kazaam, who was still clutching his old boom box, Nick paused.

"Love it, man," he said heartily. "I mean it. The whole seen-the-street look. Real world-beat." He winked at Kazaam. "You booked in, pal?" Laughing, Nick turned back to his colleagues.

Nick's associates laughed along with their boss, but Kazaam had seen his type before. As a matter of fact, it was one of his least favorite types. He gave Nick a fake, toothy grin.

"May the fleas of a thousand camels feast happily on your flesh forever," he said in perfect Arabic.

Not understanding, Nick laughed again. "Whatever you say, big guy," he said, and patted Kazaam on the arm, before going into an office down the hall.

Kazaam leaned down to nudge the still-crushed Max. "So," he said, snickering. "Who was *that* loser?"

"That was my father," Max whispered. Then he squared his shoulders and stomped out of the music club without looking back.

Kazaam stared after him. For the first time, he realized that this boy might have some problems, too.

It was later that day, and Max had to get out of the apartment. Staring miserably at his bedroom walls was just too depressing.

A few blocks away, there was a derelict garage, filled with a wilderness of rusting metal. There were rows and stacks of junked cars everywhere. It wasn't a very cheerful place, but it *was* always deserted. Whenever Max was upset, he went to the old garage to think. No one ever bothered him, and he liked looking at all of the abandoned cars.

Max threw his BMX bike down beside a heap of pickup truck beds. Then he climbed up on top of a stack of cars to sit in an old bucket seat from a long-destroyed sports car. It was his regular armchair.

Slowly, he took off the swinging dice he always wore around his neck. They had once belonged to his father, so they had always been his most prized possession. Now he didn't want them anymore.

He reached underneath the chair and pulled out an old wooden cigar box. Inside, he had hidden all sorts of special things, like his father's high school picture. There was a two-headed quarter, and a faded postcard from a trip to a tropical island. All of these were mementos from a man Max had never known.

He heard some scrap metal rattle a few feet away and glanced up sharply. It was just Kazaam, who was sitting up on top of a battered Citröen about twenty feet away.

"So, was that guy really your father?" Kazaam asked thoughtfully. "Acted like he didn't know you."

"He hasn't seen me," Max answered in a stiff voice. "In a long time. Since I was *two*, okay?"

Kazaam nodded. "Okay."

They sat quietly for a minute, and Kazaam fiddled with the knobs on his boom box.

"Uh, where'd he go?" Kazaam asked finally.

Max shrugged. "Away."

"That's a long time to be away," Kazaam observed. "I mean, it's not two or three thousand years, but . . ."

"He's back now, all right?" Max said defensively. "And things are going to be different."

"*Cool*," Kazaam responded. "But — why didn't you tell him who you are?"

Max shrugged again. "What do *you* care?"

Kazaam shrugged back at him. "Who said I *do*?"

Max had had just about enough of this irritating big guy. "Yeah, well, why don't you just leave me alone?" he asked. "I don't want you around."

Tired of trying to befriend this hostile boy, Kazaam went back into his superior genie mode. "Fine," he said, and stood up. "Is that a wish?"

"Is that all you care about?" Max asked sulkily.

His patience exhausted, Kazaam snapped right back at him. "Hey, look, bud, you're the one who called me into this mess of a world!"

Max jumped out of his chair, and slid down the pile of cars to the ground. "I didn't call anybody," he said, getting onto his bike. "Just leave me alone."

"You popped the box, so *wish*," Kazaam insisted. "Wish for a castle. A faster chariot!"

Max raced past him, fishtailing a wave of dirt over the big man.

Kazaam didn't even flinch. "I don't care what

you do!" he yelled. "*I* gotta obey the rules. I can't show my magic to anybody but you, and I can't get back in my box until you make your three wishes! So — *deal* with it!"

"Deal with *this*," Max said, and peeled away on his bike. The swift escape loosened an avalanche of scrap metal from a stack of wrecked cars.

Kazaam glowered and sidestepped the shower of metal. Then he saw a bent, rusted junior Schwinn in the pile. Growling under his breath, he straddled the small two-wheeler and pedaled after Max. He looked ridiculous as his massive feet crushed the tiny pedals.

Max led him on a makeshift obstacle course through the garage. Kazaam doggedly churned after him. He labored down a staircase of tires, pedaling furiously as his knees banged past his shoulders.

Max checked over his shoulder and was surprised to see the gigantic man right behind him. Determined to win, Max steered his bike up a plank. Then he hung a sharp right at a stop sign and smashed down onto a row of dented car hoods.

Kazaam followed him, his miniature bike lurching back and forth.

"Welcome to *my* hood, pal," Max said, and rode faster along the car hoods.

But, to Max's chagrin, Kazaam stayed right with him. In fact, he was pedaling effortlessly, with his hands folded behind his head.

"Come on, kid," he said, with a wide yawn. "At least make it hard."

Max jumped his bike off an open hood, churning down a narrow straightaway. Kazaam kept pace the whole way. Then Max stood up on his pedals, his legs moving like pistons. Slowly, but surely, he began to pull ahead.

Kazaam's tiny wheels were spinning at maximum RPMs, but he just couldn't keep up. He was so determined to win this crazy race that suddenly his tiny bike began to grow — and grow — and grow!

Max was so astonished that he almost fell off his bike. He stopped pedaling and just watched the strange scene unfold in front of him.

When Kazaam realized that his magic powers had returned, he was overjoyed.

"I'm back!" he yelled. Then he lowered his head and charged directly toward a brick wall.

"Kazaam!" Max tried to warn him. "Look out!"

Kazaam effortlessly popped a wheelie and rode straight *up* the wall.

"Take a breath, kid," he said to Max. "You gonna need it for this." Then he rode the bike straight off the top of the wall and orbited above the ruined roof of the garage. He was flying!

Max stared up at the sky, wide-eyed.

"Don't get all hysterical," Kazaam rapped happily. *"Say thank-you for your miracle!"*

Then he snapped his fingers. The boom box

vaulted right off the ground and landed in his hands. There was a puff of white smoke, and Kazaam was instantly transformed. Now he was wearing curled slippers, baggy damask pants, and an exotic vest of steel chain mail. Without a doubt, he was the best-dressed genie in town.

Max watched all of this with his mouth hanging open. It didn't seem possible, but — he had been so sure that Kazaam was lying to him about being a genie. Just in case, he closed his eyes for a second. But when he opened them, the transformed Kazaam was still pedaling up in the air, in his magically exotic outfit.

"I-I can't believe it," Max gasped finally. "You *are* a genie!"

Suddenly, his life seemed a lot more exciting than it had a few minutes ago.

7

Kazaam swooped through the air on his bike. As he passed an old neon marquee, it buzzed and sparked into life. At the same time, the boom box began to pump out music with a deep thumping bass beat.

"What'sa matter, your tongue is broken?" Kazaam chanted. *"Time like this, you should be stokin'!"* He circled over Max's head, with a wide grin on his face. *"You know the rules, now comply; Kazaam, he got — unlimited supply!"*

Max laughed as Kazaam leaned on his tin bicycle bell. First it bellowed like a foghorn. Then it sounded like a Chinese gong, followed by a duck call.

"Wait a minute," Max said, starting to catch on to what all of this meant. "You'll give me — anything? *Anything* at all?"

"Come on, boy, you're not gonna die," Kazaam rapped.

"Well, I —" Max stopped. "I mean, I'm not sure —"

Kazaam flashed behind the chimney, and he and the bike vanished in a swirl of smoke. The bicycle bell dropped forlornly out of the sky and landed at Max's feet.

Then, just as unexpectedly, Kazaam was back — and still rapping up a storm!

"Open your eyes, don't ask why, *just give it a try!"* he shouted.

Max nodded, as he started to catch the groove. *"Then I wish I had junk food, from here — to the sky!"* he said, trying to finish the rhyme.

"Why not? Higher than high!" Kazaam responded. *"You got junk food, from here — to the sky!"* He sent the bike into a tight spin and hurled the bell up into the clouds. *"I am . . . Kazaam!"*

Nothing happened.

Kazaam and Max both looked up at the empty sky.

"I *am*," Kazaam said, sounding much less certain. "Really."

Still, nothing happened. Another minute passed, and finally, a fat, sloppy cheeseburger hit Max square on the head.

Max frowned, wiping ketchup from his cheek. "That's it?" he asked. "A 'Happy Meal'?"

A handful of french fries sprinkled down like rain. Then a taco hit Max's right sneaker with a splat.

Max looked down at the mess on his shoe. "Great," he said without much enthusiasm. "That's just — great. Thanks a lot."

Up in the sky, there was a distant rumble. Another cheeseburger and two hot dogs tumbled to the ground.

"Weird," Max said. "I just — I don't know — thought it'd be *junkier*, I guess."

Kazaam looked at his hands doubtfully, and then up at the sky.

"Is that *it*?" Max asked.

Kazaam shrugged, and kept looking at the sky.

Suddenly there was a loud clap of thunder, and the heavens opened. It was a cloudburst of junk food! The sky sent down a hail of pancakes, hamburgers, burritos, and doughnuts.

"Oh, wow," Max said, and tried to run for cover.

A sheet of candy sliced down in front of him and he reversed direction. At the same time, a bolt of lightning crackled across the sky and the headlights on all of the junked cars flashed. This was starting to get dangerous!

Quickly Kazaam grabbed Max, and snatched him out of the path of a stack of steaming pizzas. The pizzas landed with a heavy thud that shook the ground.

"Whoa," Max whispered. "That was close. . . ."

Kazaam snapped his fingers and produced an umbrella out of thin air. He flicked it open and the rain of junk food bounced away from them. Max stayed within Kazaam's protective grip as the junk food pounded down all around them.

Finally, the thunder grew distant. The rain softened into a drizzle of Twinkies, Sno Balls, and Gummi Bears.

Once he was sure it was safe, Max peeked out. The garage was covered with a glistening snow of junk food.

Kazaam snapped his fingers, and the umbrella vanished. Then he folded his arms and proudly admired his feat.

Max looked around for a minute. "What?" he said finally. "No hot chocolate?"

Kazaam's face fell.

Max grinned at him. "Joke," he said — and started eating everything in sight. Never, in his wildest dreams, would he have imagined seeing so much junk food in the same place.

Kazaam watched him, looking very pleased.

"Two more!" he announced. "Make this a night you'll never forget!"

Max froze. "Wait," he said, his smile faltering. "That was a *wish*?!"

Kazaam nodded eagerly. *"Like the main man did, with da loaves and da fish!"*

Max's shoulders slumped. Were genies supposed to trick people like that? Now, he had *wasted* a wish.

"No!" he shouted. "No way! And stop rhyming!"

Kazaam shrugged. "Okay. Whatever."

Max turned away from him, thinking as hard as he could. If he only had two more, he'd better make them good ones. When he had come up with what he wanted most in the world, he turned back.

Kazaam looked eager, waiting to hear what he wanted next.

"I wish . . ." Max stopped. These words were so sincere that it was hard to say. He couldn't help feeling a little shy. "I wish my mom and dad . . . would fall back in love."

Kazaam's eagerness turned to agitation. "Love, kid? I told you. I don't *do* ethereal."

Max frowned. As far as he knew, that word hadn't exactly shown up on any of his vocabulary lists recently. "Um, ethereal?" he asked tentatively.

Kazaam sighed with great impatience. "Love, hope, talking to God, raising the dead — *you* know!" he answered. "Ethereal!"

Embarrassed by having revealed such a personal wish, Max avoided his eyes.

"But, hey," Kazaam said, putting on a salesman's happy patter. "I'm Mr. Material. And my stuff ain't too shabby. A three-story mansion? A sack o' gold? A whole land of milk and honey?" He hesitated. "I mean, you know, if that's still *in*."

Max was so busy thinking that he didn't even hear any of that.

"Come on, kid," Kazaam said restlessly. "Hurry up."

Max moved his jaw, considering that. "How long do I have to come up with the wishes?"

"*Now* would be highly advisable," Kazaam suggested, and snapped his fingers a few times. "Let's go baby, got places to go, things to do."

Max narrowed his eyes, studying this giant, jittery genie. "But I *can* wait, can't I?" he asked.

The great Kazaam hemmed and hawed — but didn't disagree with him.

Max nodded, hoping that he had the full picture now. Genie rules were new for him. "So, until I make those last two wishes, I *own* you," he said. "Don't I?"

"Well — technically," Kazaam answered grudgingly.

Max's eyes brightened. It looked like he had this genie guy right where he wanted him. He turned around and surveyed his junk food buffet.

"Well, okay," he said, and selected a Butterfinger. "Welcome to my life."

Kazaam groaned, already dreading this. If there was anything he hated, it was being told what to do. Unfortunately, that was the major part of the genie job description.

"And here's a tip, pal," Max advised. "Lose the pointy shoes."

Kazaam sat down unhappily on a pile of french fries and covered his head with his arms.

"Boy, I can't wait," Max said, and helped himself to a handful of taco chips next. There was so much to eat that he wanted to take his time. "This is going to be really *fun*."

Kazaam just groaned.

8

The next morning, Max got up bright and early. He was a guy with a mission, and his genie was going to help him accomplish it!

Kazaam hated being out in public — and he *really* hated having to follow his new, very short master around. He also wasn't too thrilled about the huge, bulky high-tops Max was making him wear, in place of his beloved pointy shoes. So he stomped sulkily down the street, lagging behind Max as much as possible.

Max headed straight for his father's nightclub, the Music Boxx. Today, he was going to do things *right*.

Unexpectedly, his watchband snapped open. His watch fell off and hit the pavement with a small crunch. Perplexed, Max picked it up. There was a fresh scratch on the crystal, and he frowned.

Ten feet behind him, Kazaam chuckled softly.

Not noticing that, Max shrugged and tucked the

broken watch into his pocket. Then he stopped short and looked down at his hand. His fingers, watch, and pocket were hopelessly ensnared in a sticky, melted pack of gum. Actually, it seemed more like *ten* melted packs.

He whirled around to face Kazaam. "Look, Godzilla," he said angrily. "I wish you'd just —"

"Wish I'd just . . . ?" Kazaam asked hopefully. "What, is that a wish?"

Max shook his head and faced forward again. He wasn't going to be tricked *that* easily!

Kazaam's eyes narrowed and he sent out a little bolt of magic with his fingers. Instantly, Max's shoelaces began knotting themselves to each other.

"Because, you know," Kazaam went on, "all you gotta do is make your last two wishes, and I'm *outta* here!"

Max tried to take a step and slammed facedown on the sidewalk with his laces locked together.

Kazaam couldn't hold back a burst of juvenile laughter. "How was your summer? Have a nice *fall*?" he asked, and then laughed even harder.

Max glared furiously at him. "Let me make this *real* clear, big guy," he said through his teeth. "You're going to do exactly what I say, and then — and *only* then — I *might* make a wish."

Kazaam stopped laughing, and started fidgeting with the dials on his boom box.

"I said, is that clear?" Max repeated himself.

Kazaam shrugged uncomfortably. "I gotta say, your whole way of thinking — truth is, it's giving me a lot of tension, kid."

"The name isn't 'kid,'" Max retorted. "It's *Max*."

They scowled at each other. Then Max broke his shoelaces apart and stamped down the street. Kazaam followed him, stamping even more fiercely.

During the rest of the walk to the Music Boxx, neither of them spoke. Once they were there, Max stood near the loading deck. Custodians were sweeping out the debris — plastic cups, streamers, crumpled napkins — from the previous night's show. Judging from the amount of garbage, there must have been a really big crowd.

Max looked at the open door, trying to get up enough nerve to go inside.

Kazaam drummed his fingers impatiently against the side of his boom box. "So," he said, his mask of cheerfulness paper-thin. "This whole I-gotta-get-the-guts-to-talk-to-Dad thing isn't gonna take *years*, is it?"

Instead of answering, Max marched right into the club without looking back. Kazaam rolled his eyes, and went after him.

Once again, there were workers all over the place, preparing for that night's gig. As one of the roadies flicked on a sampler, Kazaam stopped to listen. He nodded, liking the sound of the beat.

"Now *dis* puts da boom in da *box*," he said softly.

Intrigued, he reached over and stuck his finger on a nearby keyboard. When he pressed one of the keys, it let out a screeching bugle call.

"Cool!" Kazaam said, and he moved forward to try again.

Hassem, the burly man who had been driving the Mercedes limo the day before, grabbed his wrist. "This isn't a toy store!" he barked.

Kazaam twisted free and glared at him.

But far from being intimidated by his size, Hassem was spoiling for a fight. He clenched one fist, and motioned Kazaam forward with his other hand. "Unless you want to play *my* game," he threatened. "Come on!"

Kazaam *did* want to play that game, but he held his temper. This wasn't the right time for a fight. So he just turned his back on the fat man and walked outside into the sunshine to wait for Max.

Happy to be free of Kazaam for a while, Max explored an endless series of winding hallways and staircases in the club. Up ahead, he could hear a rocking musical beat. He turned a corner, trying to find it. Strangely, the hallway stopped short at a wall.

Max spun around and went the other way until he spotted the open door where the music was coming from. Then he heard a footstep behind him. He spun around, knowing that it must be Kazaam.

"Look, I'm getting really sick of —" He stopped when he realized that it wasn't Kazaam.

Instead, it was a young sound engineer, whose name was Ed. Ed looked at him nervously, probably wondering why there was a twelve-year-old hanging around in the club.

"Never mind," Max said lamely. "I was just leaving."

Ed shook his head. "I think you'd better come with me, kid." He grabbed Max's collar and dragged him down the hall to Nick's office.

It was a very fancy office, built around massive stereo speakers. Producers and roadies were all grooving to the beat as loud music played. Nick was giving a group of female musicians a tour of the facilities.

"It's a personal pleasure to have you ladies inaugurating 'Live in the Boxx,'" he told them. "We're going to make the hottest live recordings anyone has ever heard!"

The leader of the band looked around the room and nodded her approval. "This whole setup is dope," she said.

Standing by the doorway, Ed cleared his throat.

"Sorry to interrupt, Mr. Matteo," he said. "But this kid was in the remote booth."

Nick turned around, looking annoyed. After a moment's confusion, he recognized Max from their brief encounter the day before.

"*You!*" he said. "What are you doing here?"

Max swallowed. Standing face-to-face with his father was both scary and exciting at the same time. "I, uh — I —" he stammered.

"What's your name?" Nick demanded.

"Max," Max said hesitantly.

Nick glared at his assistants. "Who let this kid in, anyway?" he asked. "What is this, an amusement park?" He focused his attention back on Max. "Okay, Mack, the tour's over."

Max screwed up his courage. It was now or never. "It's not Mack," he answered. "It's Max. Maxwell."

"Okay, '*Maxwell*,'" Nick said sarcastically. "Now, I want you to get out of here, and —"

"*Connor*," Max said.

Nick stared at him. "Maxwell Connor?"

Max nodded tentatively.

Obviously stunned by this, Nick moved closer to him. "You're — you're my son," he said, his voice soft with wonder.

Max nodded again, still holding his breath.

His father took a sudden step back and Max cringed. But Nick was beaming as he turned toward the others.

"Everybody! This is my boy. Max. Maxwell Matteo!" he announced. Then he pointed at each of his assistants in turn. "This is Tiny. Theo. And *this* amazing wonder" — he pointed at a beautiful woman by the window — "is Asia Moon."

Asia was an exquisitely tall and slender woman.

She handed Max a tiny porcelain cup. Then, from high above him, she expertly poured him a cup of Moroccan tea.

Nick brought Max over to the next group of musicians and producers.

"Son of a gun, I don't believe this!" he kept saying. Then he draped his arm over Max's shoulders. "And you're big!" He grinned at the producers and musicians. "This is my son! How about *that*?"

The others joined in his spontaneous celebration. They all took turns clapping him on the back and giving him their congratulations

Max watched all of this with the biggest smile he had ever smiled. Whenever he had dreamed about meeting his father, it had always been *exactly* like this! Now he *knew* for sure what he had always suspected.

His father was the greatest guy in the whole world!

9

As the celebration continued, one of Nick's assistants broke out a bottle of champagne.

"What, are you crazy?" Nick asked, his arm still around Max. "He's just a boy. Get that out of here. But hey, didn't we have a pizza coming?" He winked at Max. "You like pizza, kid?"

Max nodded, feeling overwhelmed. Being with his father after so many years, and meeting all of these strangers at once, was a little hard to handle.

Nick took him over to a big leather chair. "Come on over here," he said, and hit a button on a nearby console. "Listen to this sound check."

More thumping music filled the room.

"What do you think?" Nick asked proudly. "Is this place rippin', or what?"

Max managed another nod. Somehow, he felt too shy to answer aloud.

"I still can't believe this," Nick said, and shook his head. "How old are you, anyway?"

His own father should probably know that, but

Max decided not to worry about it. "Twelve," he answered.

"Well," Nick said. "How about that."

They looked at each other. Max smiled. Nick smiled back. They looked at each other some more. Max couldn't think of anything to say, and apparently, his father couldn't, either. There was a long, uncomfortable silence.

"Well," Nick said finally, and glanced at Theo. "Where's that stupid pizza, anyway!"

The studio door burst open to reveal a huge pizza man with an armload of steaming boxes.

"Three large, two medium; Pizza Zaam's here — to bust da tedium!" the pizza man shouted. It was, of course, Kazaam, wearing a pizza delivery uniform.

As he looked for someplace to set the pizzas down, he almost bumped into the lovely Asia Moon. They exchanged stares. Then, slowly, Asia smiled.

"You *can't* be getting minimum wage," she said.

Kazaam just stared at her. In less than a second and a half, he had fallen, and fallen hard.

For the first time in thousands of years, Kazaam was in love!

When Max got home, he was still beaming from having met his father. His mother and Travis were sitting on the couch, waiting for him. They didn't look happy.

"Where have you been?" Alice wanted to know.

"Not at school, that's for sure! You're grounded, and —"

"Max, I think it's time we all had a talk," Travis said more calmly. "Let's sit down, and —"

"Hey!" Alice cut Travis off. "You just hold it! I'm not finished."

"I just think we should be reasonable," Travis told her. "Instead of —"

"Okay, whatever," Max said, as soon as he could get a word in edgewise. "I'm, uh, a little busy right now."

Before he could walk away, Alice pulled him back.

"One second, Mr. Connor," she said in a strict voice. "We're changing the way things work around here. You're going to start doing . . . chores."

What was this, *Little House on the Prairie*? Max looked at her dubiously. "Chores . . . ?" he asked. "What, milk the cows? Feed the chickens? What do you mean?"

"All right, forget chores," Travis said. "We mean, we want to help you. We're getting you a tutor. And from now on, I'm going to pick you up after school."

"No way." Max turned to his mother. "He's *not* picking me up." Then he turned to face Travis. "And I don't have to listen to you. "You're not my father. You'll *never* be my father!"

"You watch your mouth," Alice warned him.

"Watch yours!" Max retorted. "You lied to me!"

55

She hesitated, clearly not sure what he meant by that.

"You told me my father wasn't here," Max accused her. "But he is. I've *seen* him!"

It was quiet for a few seconds.

"You're right," Alice admitted quietly. "I did lie."

Max folded his arms to wait for an explanation. After all, he had missed spending a lot of years with his father. She owed him that much.

"Your father showed up two months ago," Alice said. "I didn't know what to do."

Max blinked. Only two months ago? "Well — you could have *told* me."

"Yeah," Alice said. "I could've."

There was another uneasy silence.

"Uh, how is he?" she asked.

"He's great," Max said, very defensive. "He was really nice." Then he stopped. "Why did he leave?"

Alice seemed unsure about how to answer that. "Well — he didn't," she said finally. "I did."

"But —" Max looked stunned. "Why?"

Alice struggled to find an answer. "Sometimes things just don't work out the way you plan," she said. "But I love Travis, and I want to marry him. I know I'm not the best mother, but I want you to have a real father. One who's around. Who you can count on. Do you understand?"

Max hadn't seen his mother this upset and intense for a long time. Even so, he wasn't ready to back down yet. "No," he said flatly.

Alice started to argue, but then she just gave up and shook her head. "Fine," she said, and stepped away.

Avoiding her eyes, Max went into his room and closed the door tightly. He leaned against it for a few seconds with his eyes shut. Then he went over to his closet and started searching through piles of clothes.

"So, what's 'grounded'?" Kazaam asked.

Max looked up to see Kazaam reclining among the stars on his ceiling.

"Something I'm *not*," he said. "Okay?"

Kazaam shrugged, and rested his high-tops on the Big Dipper. "If you say so."

As Max hurled clothes on the bed, Kazaam slid off the ceiling. Then he began to slither down the wall like a snake. His philosophy as a genie was to take his fun wherever and whenever he could get it.

"My dad says it's the blood that counts," Max said, thinking aloud. "So I'm going to get a job. I'll show them all!"

Kazaam nodded cooperatively.

"I'll start out as a personal assistant," Max vowed. "Then I'll show them. I mean, once I know the business and stuff. Hey, I could even have a band myself! My dad could manage us."

Kazaam paused halfway down the wall to regard Max. "Pretty big dreams, kid," he remarked.

"What would you know?" Max asked sharply. "You live in a box."

Kazaam crashed down to the floor and then dusted himself off. "Boom box, that is," he corrected Max. "So what, every once in a while, someone drags me out. And I do see things. Like a whole bunch of silly people counting on a whole bunch of silly wishes. Let me tell you, kid, the future doesn't always follow the plan."

"That's 'cause the plan stinks big time," Max said with a shrug. "See, I'm *making* my future, Kaz. And the next stop is . . ." He stopped long enough to hold up two all-access passes to that night's performance by Spinderella and KEI. "The Music Boxx!"

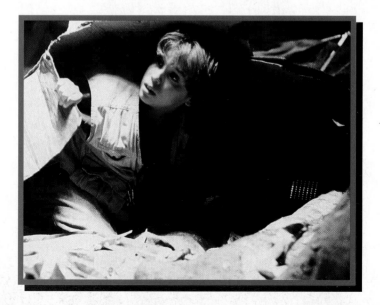

10

When Max and Kazaam got to the Music Boxx, the band was already playing. The music was jamming and the place was packed. Strobes pulsed from the ceiling, and huge monitors flashed over the crowd.

Out front, bouncers were deciding who could come in — and who *couldn't*. With their all-access passes, Max and Kazaam walked right past the velvet ropes and inside.

Kazaam was decked out as Max's fantasy of an ultra hip-hop musician. He had on a street hat, chains around his neck, and a pirate hoop in his ear. As always, of course, he was lugging his boom box.

Max was having the time of his life, but the huge crowd made Kazaam feel acutely uncomfortable. More than anything else, he wanted to go back outside and get some fresh air.

Asia Moon appeared in front of them. She looked eerily beautiful in a slinky black dress.

"Don't say I didn't warn you boys. . . ." she said with a smile. Then she turned away and disappeared into the crowd.

Kazaam hunched his shoulders a little as he looked around. "I think . . . I'm gonna wait outside," he mumbled.

Max shook his head. He was having a great time, and there was a broad grin plastered across his face. "No way, man," he shouted over the noise of the band. "This is cool!"

Suddenly, Asia came back. "Rocky? Bullwinkle?" she said pleasantly. "Shall we?"

"Yeah!" Max said.

Kazaam sighed, and followed them through the crowd.

Up above them on a balcony, Max could see his father greeting a group of V.I.P.s in a small alcove. Bodyguards and attendants were hovering nearby. Everyone's attention seemed to be focused on one person, but Max couldn't see who it was.

"This whole place, it's paradise," Max said enthusiastically to Asia. "So, like, are you and my dad really good friends?"

Asia gave him a sardonic smile. "Well, we both serve the same master," she said.

Max laughed. "What? You've gotta grant him three wishes?"

Up on the stage in the front of the room, Spinderella and KEI cranked out a hip-hop number.

The audience cheered wildly. Then Spinderella turned to the three members of KEI.

"These boys make noise, but can they ram it?" she rapped as she gestured toward the crowd.

KEI produced hand-held spotlights and used them to examine the eager members of their audience. *"I'm looking at 'em, sisters,"* one of the women in the group answered. *"Nothing but Bill-Bobs and Janets."*

Then they both turned to face the audience.

"We started this fire, think you can fan it?" they rapped in unison.

One of the rappers nailed a stone-faced man with her spotlight. *"C'mon and rap, Mr. Granite!"* she challenged him. She swung the light until it was shining on a woman with shocking red hair and lips to match. *"Drop from the tree, Lady Pomegranate!"*

Spinderella laughed, and reached for the spotlight. She waved it back and forth across the audience, looking for their next victim.

The blinding glare flicked across Max's face, and he couldn't resist waving. Then the light stopped on Kazaam.

"Who's that brother, from another planet?" she asked the crowd.

They all stared up at Kazaam's huge form, dazzled by his hip appearance. Looking embarrassed, Kazaam stepped behind Max in an attempt to hide. Since he towered over him, the attempt failed badly.

"Uh, Mega-Man?" Max said, grinning. "You're hiding an oil tanker behind a speedboat."

"You come to gawk, or you come to jam it?" KEI yelled from the stage.

The music thumped harder, and everyone waited to see what Kazaam was going to do.

"What if they don't like me?" he muttered to Max.

By now, the crowd had started jeering at him.

"They *already* don't like you," Max pointed out. Then he held Kazaam's worried eyes with a look of complete confidence. "The question is, what are you going to do about it?"

Faintly bolstered by Max's boldness, Kazaam pulled in a deep breath. "Okay," he said, and then raised his voice. *"Get set, for my tête-à-tête!"*

The audience clapped and cheered, back on his side again. To his surprise, Kazaam liked the sound even more than he would have expected.

"So tear a page from your gazette!" Spinderella called from the stage.

Kazaam jabbed his finger at her as he picked up the groove. *"The things I seen, would make you sweat,"* he rapped. *"Kings and fools, they're all fish in my net!"*

The crowd clapped their hands and swayed from side to side. They *dug* his impromptu riff.

Warming up to the idea of being a performer, Kazaam started to play to his audience.

"*'Cause I am — Kazaam!*" he yelled at the top of his lungs. *"I'm more than I seem, you're all looking at your dream. In your coffee, I'm da cream — gimme a wish, and I get extreme!"*

He raised his boom box high in the air, and a brilliant puff of light shot out. The dazzled audience ducked, but these magic "pyrotechnics" vanished in mid-flight. Encouraged by the applause, Kazaam let loose a second wave of sparks and light.

A single glowing ember from the shower of sparks flew up to the V.I.P. alcove. It landed on a lacquered table beside a mostly eaten plate of sweetbreads.

Malik, the owner of the club, paused in mid-bite. He was the same mysterious man Max had seen in the Mercedes limo a couple of days before. He was Nick's boss, and he was *not* a nice man.

"Mr. Malik, what a place," one of his dinner mates gushed. "I knew it was gonna be hot, but — *wow.*"

Malik swallowed an immense mouthful of food. His eyes never left the ember, which was glowing like an orange jewel. "I always deliver more than I promise," he said in a deep voice. Then he reached toward the ember with his fork. Like magic, the ember jumped away from him and behind a glass. Malik frowned and jabbed at the ember again. When he looked to see what he had caught, there was only his fork, stabbed deep into the table. The ember had vanished.

Malik was disappointed, but even more curious. How could a simple ember have such powers? Ignoring his dinner guests, he searched the crowd until he located the source of the sparks: Kazaam.

Unaware that he was being watched from above, Kazaam fired a last response to Spinderella and KEI.

"As Romeo said (before Juliet), grab four of your friends, we'll be a sextet!" he rapped.

"I don't know, sister," one member of KEI told Spinderella. *"He's making me sweat."*

Spinderella took up the contest. *"I got the sweat, but can this big guy slam it?"* she asked.

"If you girls are hungry, let's green eggs and ham it!" Kazaam suggested without missing a beat.

The audience cheered. On stage, Spinderella and KEI laughed. They threw him an "okay!" sign and spun into their next number.

With the excitement over, Max decided to go find his father. He headed for the V.I.P.'s alcove. Hassem, Malik's bodyguard, moved to block his way.

"I'm looking for . . . Mr. Matteo?" Max asked politely. "Sir?"

Hassem shook his head. An enormous, sleepy-eyed thug named Sam came over to join him, and they both frowned down at Max.

"Guess I'll look someplace else," Max said quickly.

Down near the stage, Kazaam was enjoying the show. Asia was standing next to him, and he smiled at her. She was just so beautiful. When she laughed a light, sweet laugh, he laughed along with her. For the first time in ages, he felt like an ordinary, love-struck human being. It was *nice.* He hoped that the feeling would never go away.

In the meantime, Max had wandered upstairs. His father had to be around someplace. His own reflection peered back at him from smoked glass windows, and stacks of amplifiers were all over the place.

He found himself in a dark, deserted corridor. At first, he was uneasy. But then, he heard voices coming from his father's office. Max started to smile, and walked more quickly. He couldn't wait to see his father again!

Before he got to the door, he heard Ed, the sound engineer, complaining.

"I didn't have any idea," Ed whined inside the office. "I didn't know we were gonna do this. I quit!"

Max peered through the doorway and saw that Ed was talking to his father. Nick looked very anxious and his face was perspiring.

"Come on, Ed, when did you suddenly get religious?" he asked. "What do you think the music business is about . . . ?"

Ed shook his head. "Not bootlegging major bands."

Max wasn't sure what "bootlegging" meant, but it certainly didn't sound good. It also didn't sound legal.

"Look," Nick said, losing his patience. "The last one of these tapes was worth a million to Malik —"

Ed interrupted him. "Piracy is a felony! I don't want to be involved!"

"You're *already* involved!" Nick shouted.

Max wished that he had never come down the hall in the first place. Unfortunately, he knew one thing for sure now — if Ed was a criminal, his father was, too!

11

Max was going to run away and pretend that he never heard the conversation, but Nick saw him.

"What are you doing here?" he demanded. "Wait outside." Then he returned his attention to Ed. "Let me paint you a picture, Ed. You *are* involved, okay? I've got fifty thousand blank CDs showing up on our little loading dock, and —" Nick stopped when he realized that Max was still standing there. "I told you to *scram!*"

Ed took advantage of the delay to make a move for the door.

"You *will* have that tape ready by three A.M.!" Nick ordered, sounding almost frantic.

"That's what you think," Ed said defiantly.

Nick grabbed him by the arms and slammed him into the wall as hard as he could. Ed winced with obvious pain, and grabbed his ribs. Nick looked down at his hands as if he were stunned by what he had just done.

Max's eyes widened and he started backing up. "You know, I think maybe I'll just go back down to the show," he said softly.

"*Stay here*," Nick told Ed. "That's an order." Then he took Max's arm and hustled him away from the office. "What're you doing up here?" he asked harshly. "You *looking* for trouble?"

Max shrank away from him. He would never have pictured his father being mean like this. "No, Dad, honest," he said, unable to keep his voice from shaking. "I just thought — I mean, you and I —"

"There *is* no you and I, kid!" his father snapped. "Got it?"

What?! "But, Dad," Max began.

"'Dad'?" Nick said, mimicking his voice. "Oh, please. I didn't raise you. I didn't play catch with you. Hey, I didn't even recognize you!" He pulled Max down the hall toward an emergency exit.

"But — the backstage passes!" Max protested. "You gave me the —"

Before he could finish his sentence, Nick had kicked the fire door open.

"Let's make it simple," his father said. "I'm *not* your dad. Not now, not ever. Now, get out of my life!"

With that, he booted Max outside. Then the fire door slammed shut, leaving Max alone and stranded on the steel fire escape.

His own father had just thrown him out like last night's garbage!

Inside, Nick ran trembling hands through his hair. What had he just done? But he had to shake this off, because he had too many other things to worry about right now. He was in way over his head.

He walked down the hall and saw two of Malik's thugs, Sam and Foad, waiting for him. Nick hesitated, then brushed roughly past them and back into his office.

Malik was already there and glaring at the hapless Ed. One by one, he was popping marzipan candy soccer balls into his mouth. The whole time, he studied Ed, who squirmed underneath his gaze.

Nick tried to break the tension with a show of breezy confidence. "Hey, boss," he said cheerfully. "I told you Spinderella and KEI would really pack the house."

"You mean, you've done your job?" Malik said, and winked at his most trusted aide, El Baz.

Nick laughed, just a little bit too late.

"Good boy," Malik said, and flipped him a piece of marzipan candy.

It tasted awful, but Nick obediently ate it. He knew better than to refuse Malik.

Malik walked over to the surveillance monitors on the wall and tapped one of the screens. "What

I'm really interested in is this man," he said, and pointed at Kazaam down on the dance floor.

"I-I don't really know," Nick stammered, not sure why Malik was interested. "He's just some guy."

Malik turned with an oily smile. "You gotta watch for these things, Nick," he said. "Gotta keep your eyes open for new talent. Gotta look for the . . . sparkle." He pinched Nick's cheek, and then headed for the door.

Nick and Ed the engineer both breathed a quiet sigh of relief.

But Malik came back over to stand in front of Ed. "Nick tells me what a good man you are," he said, and paused ominously. "I'm counting on it."

Ed gulped nervously, but managed to nod at him.

"Good," Malik said, and ate some more candy. "Glad to hear it."

Then, with one last nasty smile, he left the room.

Max took his time climbing down the fire escape. He was trying not to cry, but he couldn't help it. Down in the alley, a line of eager concert-goers was waiting to get into the club. Max squeezed through the line, not making eye contact with anyone.

"Hey!" a familiar voice yelled. "What're *you* doing here, loser?"

It was Vasquez, the gang leader from the high school. When Max looked up, he also saw Elito, Carlos, Z-Dog, and the rest of the gang standing in line.

Vasquez reached out to grab him. "I know," he said loudly. "Spinderella and KEI musta opened the show with dwarf tossing!"

Other hands reached for Max, but he broke free.

"Let go of me, you jerks!" he shouted. "Just leave me alone!"

Elito yanked at the backstage pass still dangling around Max's neck. "Where'd you find this?" he wanted to know. "Trash Dumpster?"

Max was still so angry about what his father had done that he forgot to be scared. "I was *in* there," he answered. "All right?"

The gang members laughed.

"I suppose you got a *key* to the studio?" one of them asked, and laughed even harder.

"I went all over the place," Max bragged. "I was in the V.I.P. section, even. I can go in there anytime I want. I got pull."

"Yeah, right," Z-Dog said, snickering. "Little twerp like you? Never happen."

"I'm telling the truth!" Max insisted. "They're doing a live recording worth a million bucks. They're taping it right now."

"Oh, yeah, sure," Elito said. "And you're in the video, homeboy, right?"

Tired of not having anyone respect him, Max

flared up. "Hey, if I wanted to, I could go back in there, go straight to the recording booth, and put the tape right in your hands!" he responded.

Most of the gang hooted at this, but Vasquez had stopped laughing now.

"You mean that, homie?" he asked thoughtfully.

"Yeah," Max said, looking him straight in the eye. "I sure do."

Vasquez rubbed his hands together, already mentally counting the money they were going to make. "Okay, then," he said greedily. "Then I think you and me are going to have ourselves a little talk."

Max gulped. Somehow, that didn't sound very good. . . .

12

When the show was over, a crowd of fans gathered around the row of limos waiting to take Spinderella and KEI and their entourage to their hotel. Spinderella and KEI strutted outside to the sound of cheers.

Kazaam walked out behind them. He had been looking everywhere for Max, but he couldn't find him. Where could he have gone? It had been hours.

To his surprise, a group of fans swarmed around him. At first, he looked for a way out. But it turned out that all they wanted was to congratulate him on his performance. So Kazaam relaxed and started shaking hands with everyone. If this was what fame was like he could *definitely* get used to it!

Inside one of the Mercedes stretch limos, Malik watched Kazaam awkwardly sign autographs. Asia was sitting next to him in the limousine. Malik noticed that she was watching Kazaam, too.

"Like what you see?" he asked.

"Him?" Asia answered dismissively. "He's *tall*, Malik. Don't mistake that for interesting."

"I was raised to find everything interesting," Malik said. "He's got a secret bigger than he is. Know a person's secret, you own them, right, Asia?"

Asia shrugged, and looked down at her hands instead of answering.

Malik reached over and opened the limo door for her. "Go bring me his secret," he ordered.

Swallowing her reluctance, Asia slowly got out of the car. She hated following orders. But she waved one hand to catch Kazaam's attention.

"Malik would like you to join us tonight," she said, and indicated the limo.

Kazaam thought that sounded great, but he hesitated. "I don't know if I should. Thing is, I'm kind of looking for Max," he said.

"Oh, he's with Nick," Asia lied. "I think we'd just be in the way."

That made sense to Kazaam. Max and his father had a lot of catching up to do. So he picked up his boom box and followed her over to the limousine.

Inside the car, Malik was drinking expensive champagne. His driver had lit some incense, which gave the limo an exotic smell. Malik offered Kazaam a brass bowl filled with what looked like marbles.

Kazaam stared, unable to believe what he was

seeing. "Nubian goat eyes?" he asked enthusiastically.

Malik nodded. "The food of kings."

"Wow!" Kazaam said, and started helping himself. "Haven't had these in three thousand" — he caught himself before he said *years* — "*days*," he said. "Thanks."

Malik watched him eat. "You have old-fashioned tastes," he observed.

Kazaam stopped chewing, not sure what he meant by that. "Well, I, uh, don't get out much," he said finally.

"That, we can change," Malik promised.

Kazaam looked at Malik, looked at Asia, and then smiled.

"Sounds good to me," he said, and took another handful of goat eyes.

What he didn't notice was the way Malik was enviously studying his boom box. He also didn't know that what Malik wanted, Malik *got*.

After the last fans had faded into the night, the lights went out at the Music Boxx. A light wind was blowing, and discarded flyers and old tickets flew through the air. It was very dark. Soon, a large truck pulled up to the loading dock behind the building.

In a shadowy doorway, Vasquez watched the loading dock door roll up. He had one hand clamped tightly around Max's shoulder. The rest of the gang was hiding nearby. As soon as they got a chance, they were going to steal the tape from the concert.

Nick was standing on the loading dock, directing the action. His assistant began unloading pallets of gleaming metal cylinders. Malik had ordered Nick to make bootleg CDs of tonight's concert. It would be cheating Spinderella and KEI and the record company, but Malik would make at least a million dollars from the crime. There was a high-tech security camera running above them, recording every step of the operation.

Nick pointed at a yellow square painted on the cement. "Put them here," he said, "inside the lines."

The crew did exactly what he told them to do.

Vasquez signaled to the rest of the gang that it was time to get ready. Soon, they would make their move! Max was going to have to help, whether he liked it or not.

The crew of assistants grunted and groaned as they wrestled the heavy pallets into position. When they were looking the other way, Vasquez and the gang dashed through the open door. They all, including Max, hid behind boxes and crates.

Once the truck had been unloaded, Nick handed the men thick rolls of cash. As they drove off, he punched a red button. The loading dock door began to rumble down.

Nick stepped onto the first pallet and waved at the security camera. A hidden freight lift started to move below him. It carried Nick and the pallet of blank CDs up toward an innocent-looking shaft in the ceiling.

Ed came into the loading bay. He was carrying the master tape of the concert.

"Wait here," Nick advised. "Ride up with the second pallet."

Ed didn't seem to like the idea of being alone with the valuable tape, but he nodded. Just as Nick and the pallet disappeared into the air shaft, two figures burst out of the darkness. One body-blocked Ed, while the other tried to wrestle the tape out of his hand. Ed fought as hard as he could, but two more gang members jumped on top of him.

Max stared at the lowering loading dock door, and then at the fight. Should he run away, call for help, or just hide until it was over?

The rest of the gang was struggling to subdue the engineer, so Vasquez leaped into the fight. With one fierce blow, he knocked Ed out. He and the rest of the gang scrambled off the pallet. Elito was clutching the master tape now, and he zipped it inside his jacket to keep it safe.

"Let's get out of here!" Vasquez shouted.

The gang members darted toward the slowly descending door.

Max stood right where he was, frozen in place. Was Ed hurt, or just stunned? Should he help him? He really didn't know what to do.

Just then, Sam and Foad, two of Malik's burly bodyguards burst through a door. They both started throwing punches. Someone screamed, and Vasquez lunged off the floor to smash the only light. Now the whole loading bay was covered with darkness.

In the resulting chaos, Max was the last one out. He barely managed to roll under the door as it slammed shut. He lay on the cold cement, trying to catch his breath.

Behind him, a small door opened. Sam and Foad charged outside, screaming threats and swinging metal pipes. The gang members quickly scattered, but Sam and Foad chased them. If they caught any of the thieves, they would kill them!

Hearing the men panting right behind him, Max dove behind a Dumpster. He huddled on the ground, covering his head with his arms. He was so scared and shaking all over that he could barely breathe. He could hear footsteps pounding everywhere.

If Sam and Foad found him, he would be lucky to escape with his life!

13

Max hid behind the Dumpster for a long time. When it was finally quiet, he crept out. Sam and Foad must have given up and gone back inside. He was safe! Being part of a robbery had been terrifying, but it had also been kind of exciting. He would worry about how to get the master tape back tomorrow.

When he got home, he found his mother asleep on the living room sofa. She must have been worried about him. He wanted to let her know he was home safely, but she looked too peaceful. Besides, if he woke her up, he knew he would confess everything and that would only make her worry more.

He was too tired to change into pajamas. So he fell asleep in his clothes. He woke up early the next morning when he felt an immense arm flop across his chest.

It was Kazaam, who was blissfully murmuring a mix of Arabic and English to himself.

"Oh, I feel good," he mumbled, still sound asleep.

Max tried to get up, but he was pinned by the weight of Kazaam's arm. "Hey, come on," he said. "Move!"

Kazaam stretched, and to Max's amazement, Kazaam began to grow. The blankets and pillow started growing, too!

"Hey!" Max protested, as the blanket went over his head like a tidal wave. "Get out of here, Kazaam! Go grow someplace else!"

"I'm more than I seem," Kazaam rapped in his sleep. *"In your coffee, I'm da cream! I feel . . . extreme!"*

Max hit him with his now-gigantic pillow. "Wake up already!" he yelled. "You're way too big!"

Kazaam opened his eyes, and shot out of bed. He began to rebound off the walls until he was back to his normal huge size, instead of being super-sized.

"You know, you were right to get me out there last night," he said happily. "They totally loved me!"

Max stared at him. Since when had his genie been so *cheerful*? It was kind of annoying.

Kazaam stopped bouncing long enough to marvel at Max's constellation-speckled ceiling. "Was this here yesterday?" he chirped. "Look — Virgo! Aw, Max, you should've *seen* this party I went to! We were in Malik's limo, chillin', with goat eyes!"

Max made a face. Goat eyes sounded more gross than fun.

Kazaam ping-ponged off the ceiling and over to Max's desk. He peered down at an open junior chemistry book, with a page of half-scrawled equations next to it. " 'Polar covalent bonds have an ionic — ' " He stopped reading. "Hey, you know this stuff, little guy?"

Max slapped the book shut. "My mom wishes I did," he said grimly.

Now Kazaam noticed Max's vacuum-cleaner motor project. He had hot-wired the motor with sizzling speaker-wire, and a ball bearing was floating above it, trapped in a magnetic field.

"Wow!" Kazaam said with a big grin. "You're a genie, too!"

Max was in such a lousy mood that he didn't smile back. "Why don't you take a shower or something," he grumbled. "What's the matter, can't materialize soap?"

A gleam came into Kazaam's eyes. Then a shower of water burst into life in the middle of the room. Max scrambled to safety as Kazaam lathered up with a ten-pound bar of Safeguard. Luckily, the suds and water evaporated before they hit the floor.

"Your dad's so lucky to work with this Malik guy," Kazaam said, as he scrubbed away. "He said I got a future in the biz. Is Asia gonna love me or what?"

The shower vanished and two spa towels appeared out of thin air to dry Kazaam's ears.

"*Especially* now that I'm all clean and sparkly," he said. He snapped his fingers, and the towels were gone. Then he sat down on the bed, finally ready to hear about Max's adventures. "So, you and your dad have a nice night, too?"

"Oh, yeah," Max said, scowling. "It was terrific."

Before Kazaam had time to ask him what was wrong, they heard Alice's cheerful voice.

"Max!" she called from the kitchen. "French toast!"

"*Rôtie Française?*" Kazaam said, using a heavy French accent. "I love it *beaucoup!*"

Max just walked out of the room with his shoulders slumped.

For the first time, Kazaam was genuinely concerned. But until Max came back, there wasn't much he could do about it. So he stretched out on the bed to wait, with his long legs hanging over the end.

Max sat down at the kitchen table without saying good morning. Alice handed him a glass of orange juice, but he didn't move or look up.

"That's right," his mother said in a hearty voice. "It's poisoned."

Usually that would have made Max smile, but he didn't.

"I figured if you ended your suffering, mine

would end, too," Alice explained. She was trying to jolly him out of his bad mood, but so far, it wasn't working.

Defiantly, Max downed the entire glass of juice.

"That's my boy," Alice said, and then she tousled his hair. "And could my boy please do me one favor? Don't run away anymore."

Max shrugged, instead of answering.

"Here," Alice said, handing him a platter of French toast. "I made your favorite. With chocolate chips, *and* peanut butter."

Max pushed the plate away. "I'm not hungry," he said.

Alice sighed. "For once in your life, let me have the last word, okay?"

She got up and opened the refrigerator to get some more juice. As she turned back to the table, she screamed.

Max looked up to see Kazaam standing in the hallway. He was dressed in a conservative jacket and slacks, a sweater vest, and a plaid bow tie.

"Sorry, so sorry," Kazaam said smoothly. "Max insisted. He's told me so much about you."

Alice gawked at the immense young man as he sat down at the table. "Have I — met you before?" she asked.

"No, ma'am," Kazaam answered, pouring himself some juice. "I am Jefferson Allensworth Lamb. Jefferson, for the man who framed our fine constitution. Allensworth, for he who founded a community of free blacks. And Lamb, because I like to eat lamb chops."

Max and Alice stared at him, both of their mouths gaping open.

Alice was the first to recover herself. "Uh, yes," she said, still confused. "So, you're Max's . . . friend?"

Kazaam-Jefferson gave her a toothy smile. "Kind of you to call me a friend, but the school district more commonly refers to me as a tutor," he said.

"Tutor?" Alice asked, and checked her watch. "I'm sorry, I didn't hear you come in."

"We wanted to get an early start," Max explained. "I'm, uh, pretty far behind."

Alice looked at him suspiciously. Probably because he had never been so gung ho about school?

"Well," Kazaam-Jefferson said, and stood up. "We'd better get moving, young man, or you'll be late for class."

Max nodded. "You're right," he said. "Can't have that."

"Certainly not," Kazaam-Jefferson agreed. "Hustle up, son. Lovely to meet you, ma'am."

"Uh, you, too," Alice said.

"Go get all of your books," Kazaam told Max sternly. "I also want to see three freshly sharpened pencils, a ruler, your compass, and a yellow Hi-Liter."

"Right away!" Max promised, and he headed for his room.

From the corner of his eye, Max could see his mother watching all of this with some confusion. She clearly didn't recognize this new and improved academic version of him — but she obviously liked what she saw!

14

Max and Kazaam took their time walking to school together. Max was worrying about everything that had happened the night before, while Kazaam was just enjoying the delightful weather. Max knew he needed some advice, but he wasn't sure how to ask for it.

"I, um, I was wondering something," he ventured hesitantly. "I mean — well —"

Kazaam shrugged, grooving to a beat that only he could hear. "Spit it out, kid," he said. "You know me — I protect, and I serve."

"I just — if someone were to take something that wasn't really his, but no one got hurt," Max said slowly. "That's not so bad, is it?"

Kazaam shrugged. "I don't know. Depends on the taker and the takee."

"What about you?" Max asked. "You ever taken anything you shouldn't have?"

Kazaam looked guilty. "Uh, me?" he asked.

"Yeah, you," Max said.

Instead of elaborating, Kazaam wandered down a nearby alley to avoid the issue entirely. The brick walls were thick with graffiti, and rusting fire escapes hung from each building. Overhead, cast-off clothes dangled on frayed clotheslines. But it was a dead end, and Kazaam had no place to go. He turned around to face Max.

"Come on, what's the worst thing you ever did?" Max pressed him.

Kazaam let out a heavy sigh. "Look, kid, shouldn't you be in school?" he asked. "Learning yourself a lot of new stuff? Because I, uh, I got things to see, people to do."

"What?" Max wanted to know. "What things?"

"I, um, gotta get ready," Kazaam mumbled.

Max wasn't sure what he was talking about. "Ready for what?" he asked blankly.

"Well, uh, for tonight," Kazaam said, looking embarrassed. "I'm gonna perform."

Max couldn't help being surprised by that. "Oh, come on. *You?*"

"Hey, you said I was cool," Kazaam reminded him defensively.

"Okay," Max said, half-amused and half-doubtful. "Why not? So, what are you going to rap about?"

Kazaam lifted his shoulders in a helpless shrug. "Tell you the truth, I got a little tension about this whole thing," he admitted. "And you only get one shot. I mean, I can't even get my threads straight, you know?"

"It doesn't matter what you wear," Max said. "It's your rap. Your rhymes. You have to have something to say. Like this." Max struck a cool pose, demonstrating the way he thought Kazaam should act.

"Give me a break, kid. What do *you* know about rappin'?" Kazaam asked.

"*My name is Max, get these facts,*" Max responded. "*On my heavy BMX, I make some tracks!*"

Rising to the challenge, Kazaam flicked on his boom box. The sounds of percussion and a pounding bass-line filled the air.

"You do better," Max encouraged him.

Kazaam thought for a few seconds, listening to the beat of the music. "*My name is Kazaam, I got the whole plan,*" he started tentatively. "*So listen to the man, I'm the sultan of sand.*" He stopped, looking at Max for approval.

"*Is that it, is that the whole deal?*" Max asked, egging him on. "*You want to be a hit, you better get real.*"

Kazaam nodded, starting to remember how to do it. Then he vanished and appeared in the middle of a laundry line of lingerie.

"*I have this friend, in one thousand B.C.,*" he said, tearing into the rhythm. "*We discovered a bevy, of bathing beauties. Hbur looks to me, and I says to he, why don't we jump, in that old Euphra-tes?*"

Max nodded, enjoying the way the story was

unfolding. *"So that's the whole story?"* he rapped. *"That's all you gotta tell?"*

Kazaam stepped through the hanging lingerie. Now he was wearing his genie vest and pants. *"You gotta listen to my rap, from bell to bell,"* he said.

Now the boom box music began to magically change from a hip-hop rhythm to the Arabic sound of pipes, harmoniums, and drums.

"Those babies had rabies, we was in Hades," Kazaam went on enthusiastically. *"'Cause we moved with da harem, of Prince Akba D'Karem!"*

Trash-can lids in the alley began to pound the beat. Suddenly, Max found himself dressed as a sultan with a stick as a sword. He liked genie magic!

"So it's you and Hbur, in one thousand B.C.," he prompted Kazaam.

"Buried to our necks, in sand like a sea," Kazaam rapped on. *"By a Sultan with a sword, and a lock and a key!"*

"They're in it deep," Max observed. *"Will they ever get free?"*

"And I looks to Hbur —" Kazaam said.

"And he says to thee —" Max chimed in.

"Come the end of this day, we ain't gonna be!" Kazaam finished the rap.

The alley magically split into two worlds, the present and the past. The present-day Max and Kazaam clutched each other in fear as they watched the "story" Max and Kazaam get buried up to their chins in the sand.

"So *it's me and Hbur, in one thousand* B.C.," Kazaam rapped. *"Praying to the gods —"*

"And what do you see?" Max asked.

In the past world, a "story" Max appeared with a scepter and an aluminum casserole dish on his head.

"A man with a halo, and a nasty decree," Kazaam said, watching the past world unfold before them. *"I'll save your butts, but you gonna serve me!"*

As they watched in horror, the "story" Max and Kazaam were now buried up to their *noses* in sand.

"I nod to Hbur, and he nods to me," Kazaam rapped. *"And when the magic is over, we ain't men —"*

"We genie!" Max and Kazaam yelled together.

The "story" Max and Kazaam burst out of the sand. They were both dressed as genies now.

"We were buried to our necks, in sand like a sea," they rapped together. *"By a sultan with a sword, and a lock and a key! And I looks to Hbur, and he says to me, 'We ain't men, we genie!'"*

"What are we, Max?" Kazaam asked with one big hand cupped to his ear.

"We genie!" Max answered.

"I can't hear you, Max, I cannot hear you," Kazaam rapped. *"What are we?"*

"We genie!" they both yelled at the top of their lungs.

The rap was over now, and they both burst out

laughing. They exchanged high fives. Then there was a flash, and the two worlds merged. The past was gone, and they were both back in their street clothes again.

Max started clapping. "Man, it must be great to be a genie," he said enthusiastically.

Kazaam shrugged. "Sure it is," he conceded, "but — you're locked up. A couple of millennia later, your lamp breaks. You think you're free, but you're sucked into a compass. You go down with the ship."

Max sat down on the curb, realizing that this was a true story.

"One day, you're salvaged," Kazaam went on. "You wind up in a clock, a trombone, a radiator, and — you got it — a boom box." He shook his head. "Ever hear of slavery?"

Max had never thought about it that way before. "But, you can just snap your fingers and have anything," he said.

"Oh, yeah?" Kazaam asked, and then shook his head again. "Can't make myself free. Can't make someone fall in love. I can't even *touch* destiny. Hey, I can't even make someone fall in love with *me*!"

"I wish — I wish *I* could change things," Max said with genuine emotion. "Make things different."

Kazaam didn't answer, since he wished the very same thing.

"I'm sorry," Max said. "I didn't realize how hard it is for you."

"You weren't talking about genies, anyway," Kazaam told him. "You're talking about Djinn."

"Djinn?" Max asked, not sure if he was pronouncing it right. "What's a Djinn?"

Kazaam's eyes got distant. "A Djinn is *free*," he said softly. "A Djinn can do anything. Love. The future. Fate." Then he returned his wistful gaze to Max. "The problem is, Max — Djinn only exist in fairy tales."

"I don't believe in fairy tales, either, Kazaam," Max admitted. "But then again, I didn't believe in wishes."

"And look what you got," Kazaam said wryly.

If he ever got a chance to make another wish, Max was going to wish as hard as he could for Kazaam to be free.

15

For the next few minutes, they sat there in the alley in friendly silence. Then Kazaam tilted his head to one side, listening intently.

"Your school have a bell?" he asked.

Max checked his watch. He was already late. "Oh, man, I'd better get going. See you later."

"Okay. See ya," Kazaam answered.

As Max hurried away, Kazaam glanced at his own watch and cringed. If he wasn't careful, *he* would be late, too!

Max was hurrying down the hallway at school when he heard noisy steps behind him. He turned, ready to make an inventive and amusing excuse to the hall monitor. But it was Vasquez and the gang. Max sighed, and got ready to defend himself yet again.

"Hey, man!" Carlos said, and high-fived him. "What's happening?"

"Yo, it's the *business man*," Z-Dog added. "How you doin'?"

He wasn't sure why, but for some reason, the gang seemed happy to see him. In case they were bluffing, he stayed very alert.

"So," Vasquez said, slinging his arm around Max's shoulder. "You gotta talk to your dad. Tell him if he wants the tape, it's gonna cost him."

"How much?" Max asked nervously.

Vasquez mulled that over. "Don't worry, we'll work something out."

Max didn't say anything. The idea of extorting money from his father — even though he seemed to be kind of a jerk — made him uncomfortable.

"So, this is your big chance, kid," Vasquez said, sounding like a friendly older brother. "Do this — and everything changes. You got money, everybody looks at you differently. You *don't* do this, and . . . " He let his voice trail off dangerously. "Hey, you don't want to say 'No,' know what I mean? You think you're man enough, kid?"

Max, frankly, had no idea if he was man enough or not. But he was willing to try. "Fine. Just tell me what you want," he said.

"*Outstanding*," Vasquez said, and led him into the nearest bathroom to explain *exactly* what he wanted.

*　　*　　*

Down at the Music Boxx, everyone was hard at work when Max arrived. As usual, they had a new show to put on that night.

When the stage manager saw Max at the door, he lowered his clipboard.

"Hey, we're not —" He stopped, recognizing who it was. "Oh, hey, Max. How are you?"

Max gave him a nervous nod and marched upstairs to meet his father. The sooner he told his father about the tape, the sooner all of this might be over. He wished that he had never gotten involved in the first place.

He was halfway down the hall when his father's door came crashing open. Max jumped out of the way just as Nick was hurled forcefully through the doorway and landed on the hard floor with a thud.

Lying flat on his stomach, Nick couldn't see his son. Before Max could react, Sam, the thug, swaggered out to the hall. Max quickly hid behind the open door where he wouldn't be seen.

"Up," Sam said to Nick, and then he prodded him with his heavy boot. "Come on, get up."

Max held his breath, terrified. He darted to look to one side and saw Malik's cruel face through the crack in the doorjamb. Were they just trying to scare his father, or were they going to kill him?

With frightening ease, Sam grabbed Nick and threw him back into the office. Max watched in horror as Sam and Hassem both punched him a few times.

Then Malik reached down and helped the gasping Nick to his feet.

"Nick, Nick," he said, looking genuinely pained. "You *knew* the tape was worth a million dollars. What were you thinking? You were gonna work it off?"

"I-I —" Nick struggled to get his breath. "I know how much it was worth, sir. I'll find it."

"All right. But what will *I* find?" Malik asked, shaking his head sadly. "My loyal friend Nick? Or a man at the bottom of the lake?"

"Don't worry, I'll bring you the tape by midnight," Nick promised.

"I hope so," Malik said, and he folded his arms across his chest. "But I still find it curious. On the surveillance tapes, it looks like we were robbed by a bunch of little boys. How could that be?"

Nick shrugged uneasily. "I don't know. Really."

"Neither do I, my friend," Malik said, with the threat obvious in his voice. "Neither do I. But, believe me, I'm going to find out. . . . "

Max crept down the hall, making sure that no one saw him. Then he raced downstairs at top speed and through the back door of the club. His father needed help, and Max only knew one person he could ask.

Running as hard as he could, Max slipped behind the cover of a couple of trash Dumpsters. It

was the same place he had hidden the night before, and he knew it was safe.

"Kazaam!" he whispered, between gasping
breaths. "Help, Kazaam, I need you! Kazaam!!"

There was no response.

"Kazaam, help!" Max pleaded. "If you can hear
me, I need help! Kazaam!"

What good was a genie if he was never around
when you needed him?

"Please, Kazaam, I need help!" he begged. "If
you can hear me, please help! Kazaam!"

There was still no answer.

16

As it happened, Kazaam was on a date. He had agreed to take Asia Moon to lunch. They were eating at a hip, crowded spot called the Union Station Grill. Kazaam was doing his very best to impress this vision of beauty sitting across the table. He couldn't ever remember being so nervous.

He was in the middle of a story when he felt a strange, sharp twitch in his ear. He shook it off, and went on with the tale.

"Anyway, Paul Revere's ready, but he doesn't have a horse," Kazaam said, gesturing dramatically. "So he wishes for the fastest mare in creation, and what do you know? A new country's born!"

"Where did you learn all this?" Asia asked, looking awed. "Harvard?"

Kazaam wished that he could tell her the truth about his life, but he knew that he couldn't. She would never believe it, and she also might lose interest in him. "Harvard?" he repeated. "I'm too smart for Harvard. I experienced my academia, in Upper Mesopotamia! But, I got my major, in the Mysteries of Asia."

Asia smiled. She seemed touched by his playful charm.

"I'm just the girl next door," she said, sipping some iced tea. "But *you*, you're interesting. Tell me more."

Kazaam's twitch reappeared, more strongly. He shook his head a few times, then jammed his finger in his ear until the twitch went away.

"I've lived in a lot of neighborhoods over the years, Asia, and believe me, you were *never* next door," he said with a wink. "How'd you get to work for a great guy like Malik, anyway?"

Asia shook her head. "Believe me, you don't want to know."

"Yes, I do," Kazaam insisted. "Tell me."

"With a talent like yours, you'll get to know him as well as I have," she said, rather bitterly. She pushed aside her salad plate and reached for her purse. "Excuse me, I'll be right back."

Kazaam stood up politely from the table as she left. Then he sat down and lifted his water glass. He was about to take a large sip when he saw a tiny image of Max shouting in the water.

Startled, Kazaam dropped the glass and it shattered all over the table. Max found himself sitting on the table, stunned and totally *soaked*. He looked around the restaurant, not sure where he was, or how he had gotten there. The last thing he remembered was being in the alley and calling out Kazaam's name.

"Hey, get off the table, Max!" Kazaam protested. He took out his napkin and tried to wipe up the water. "Come on! I'm on a date, fool."

"I'm sorry, Kaz, but I gotta make a wish," Max said frantically.

Hearing the urgency in his voice, Kazaam looked worried, too. "Right now?" he asked, glancing around to see if Asia was on her way back yet.

Max rolled his eyes impatiently. "No, in two hundred and fifty years," he said. "What do you think? Kazaam, I need a tape. No —" He stopped and shut his eyes. "I *wish* I had the tape."

Nothing happened, and he opened his eyes.

"What's wrong with you?" he asked, struggling not to lose his temper. Wasn't Kazaam paying attention to him? "I made a wish!"

Kazaam cocked his head to one side, looking confused. "Well, what kind of tape?" he asked.

Shouldn't a genie be able to read his mind? "The master tape of last night's show," Max said. "Please, that's all I want."

Kazaam shrugged. "What's the big deal? Can't your dad give it to you?"

Max fixed him a cold stare. "Do you have a problem with this wish?" he asked.

"Uh, no," Kazaam assured him. "It's just — it's your second wish."

"So?" Max asked pugnaciously.

"So — I don't know," Kazaam said. "You want to waste it on some dumb *tape*?"

"Yes!" Max said, and pounded his fist on the table for emphasis. "I do!"

Kazaam frowned at him curiously. "Why?"

"Don't argue with me, just get me the tape!" Max barked at him. "Come on, come on, you know the drill. 'I am — Kazaam!' Let's go!"

Kazaam pursed his lips, deep in thought. Then he grinned, and snapped his fingers. He vanished with such a sudden vortex that the tablecloth was yanked out from under the food. His disembodied hand tapped Max's shoulder, and Max felt his hair stand on end.

"No!" he shouted.

Just then, he felt himself spin out of control, and disappear!

Max tumbled back into existence in the sound booth at the Music Boxx. His hair was smoking and he looked like he'd been on a roller coaster ride through hell.

He sat up, feeling dazed. "What are we doing *here*?" he asked.

"Saving you a wish, m'man," Kazaam said cheerfully. He riffled through a rack of tapes, searching for the Spinderella and KEI recording.

Max scrambled up and rushed to his side. "It's not here," he muttered.

101

"How do you know?" Kazaam asked, and kept searching. "Be patient."

"I just know, okay!" Max said.

Hearing the panic in his voice, Kazaam lifted an eyebrow at him. "*Why* isn't the tape here?" he asked.

Feeling boxed in by all of the questions, Max jabbed a finger into Kazaam's chest. "Why are you stalling?" he asked angrily. "All you ever wanted was for me to make three wishes, remember?"

Kazaam retreated a couple of steps, worried that Max might be right. When he spoke, his voice was gentle. "Talk to me, Max," he said. "I'm your buddy. . . . "

Max felt too frustrated and guilty to see anything beyond his immediate need. "Forget it, I don't need a friend!" he snapped. "I need a genie. Now grant my second wish. I *order* you."

There was a tense silence.

Kazaam's whole face fell — and then his expression hardened. "Fine," he said through his teeth. "Your wish is my command."

Slowly, Kazaam clenched his fist and brought it smashing down on the boom box. Bursts of magical energy spurted through a crack in the side of the machine. Then the master tape appeared between them, slowly spinning in the air.

Max and Kazaam stared at each other. They both knew they had gone too far, but they were also both too stubborn to admit it.

102

Max snatched the tape from the air. "I'm out of here," he said stiffly.

Kazaam scowled at him. "Allow me," he offered.

"Oh, yeah," Max said. "Do it."

As the words came out of his mouth, Max realized that it was dumb to mess with your genie. In the next instant, his hair stood straight out, and just like that, before he had a chance to scream, he was gone!

17

Max tumbled back into the world right in the middle of Mrs. Duke's social studies class. He rubbed his eyes, and shook his head to clear it. Mrs. Duke was standing up at the board, asking her bewildered class questions they couldn't seem to answer.

"So, who can tell me at least four of the republics of the former Soviet Union?" she asked, her voice sounding quite strained.

She turned away from the board to see Max, sitting in the last row, with his hair electrified. "Ah, Max," she said, looking relieved. "Good for you!"

Max's eyes swiveled and narrowed as he discovered that his arm was already raised. It must have been Kazaam's revenge.

"Well?" Mrs. Duke asked, waiting at the board with her chalk poised.

"Ah," Max racked his brains, trying to think. He hadn't been doing his homework for the last few days, and he was completely lost. "Unocal," he said, taking a shot in the dark. "Unistan. Pakistan."

Mrs. Duke frowned at him over her glasses, and he knew that he hadn't even come close.

"Stan the Man?" he guessed.

Mrs. Duke moved her jaw. Then the only word she wrote on the board was DETENTION.

Over at the Music Boxx, Malik was sitting in the V.I.P. alcove, enjoying a large lunch. He was the only one eating, but there was enough food for five people on the table. Around him, the rest of the club was empty except for a two-man crew testing stage lights.

Asia, accompanied by El Baz, walked across the empty dance floor.

Seeing her, Sam quickly brought over a chair and set it across from Malik.

Excited, Malik looked up from his buffet. A stack of delicious boiled sweetbreads was impaled on his fork, but that could wait.

"Tell me you had a wonderful breakfast!" he exclaimed. "Tell me you couldn't eat another bite. In fact, tell me . . . everything!"

Asia shrugged and sat down. The last thing she wanted to do was cooperate with Malik's devious plan. She checked her earrings, and then put on another funkier pair. "LSU grad, professional performer, started when he was seven," she recited in a bored voice. "As I said, the only interesting thing about him is his height."

Malik squinted at her with fierce eyes. "You're a good looker," he said. "But not a good liar."

Asia tensed her muscles, wondering what he was going to do next. Malik was famous for his short temper.

"Come on, Asia," Malik said, sounding pleasantly threatening. "Give Kazaam another shot, won't you? I *know* there's something funny about that boom box. And I'm just *dying* to find out!"

From the way he said it, Asia knew that if she didn't find out, she might end up dying, too.

As soon as detention was over, Max raced outside to get his bike. He was about to jump on when a hand locked on his arm. Max spun around to see — his father.

"Dad!" he gasped. "I mean — hi!"

Nick forcibly guided him toward his car. "We gotta talk," he said. "Come on."

Just as Nick shoved Max into a dark Cadillac, Max spotted his mother charging out of a taxi and racing toward them. Before Nick could get in on the driver's side, Alice yanked the passenger door open and tried to pull Max out.

"Max, get out of the car!" she said sharply. "Right now."

Nick shook his head, and held on to Max so he would stay inside. "Unh-unh, no way."

She stared at him. "Nick? Just what exactly do you think you're doing?" she asked.

"This is between me and my boy," he answered. "You stay out of it."

"*Your* boy?" Alice asked, a sneer in her voice. "You haven't seen him in a decade! You have no rights here!"

Nick sighed. "Look, this has nothing to do with you, Alice."

"Oh, really? You want me to call the cops?" she asked. "I will." She turned to Max. "And *you*, get out of this car at once."

Max shook his head, staying right where he was.

"What's the matter with you?" Alice demanded. "This is your mother speaking, Maxwell! Now, come on!" She grabbed his shirt, but he twisted away from her.

"Let go!" he yelled. "Just — go back to Travis!" That must have shocked her because she released her grip on his shirt. "Max —" she started.

Max hunched down in his seat, refusing to look at her. "Stop pretending you care!" he said.

Alice just stared at him.

Nick didn't wait for her to recover. He just turned on the ignition and stomped on the accelerator. Alice jumped back as the Cadillac swerved away from the curb.

She tried to run after the car, but Nick swiftly left her in the dust.

Max stared back over the seat at the receding figure of his mother. Her shoulders were slumped and she looked miserable. He hadn't wanted to hurt her feelings, but the last thing he needed was for her to get in the middle of all this trouble. Being rude to her had seemed like the best way to keep her safe.

He just hoped that when he told her the truth, she would be able to forgive him.

He also hoped that he would be able to forgive himself. . . .

18

Nick glared out through the windshield as he drove. He was gritting his teeth, and the muscles in his jaw kept clenching every few seconds.

Max looked at him, trying to figure out a way to talk about the master tape.

"In twenty years —" Nick began. Then he started over. "No, actually, never in my whole *life* have I ever seen anything so stupid."

"What?" Max asked, completely baffled. "What are you talking about?"

Nick took his right hand off the wheel long enough to shake it at him. "Don't lie to me!" he snapped. "I know what you stole, you and your punk friends!"

First of all, Vasquez and the gang weren't exactly his friends. And second, how could his father possibly know that he had been involved at all?

"I-I didn't," Max said weakly. "I mean —"

"I thought I told you not to lie to me! Do you realize what you did?" Nick asked, and then shook his head with both fury and disgust. "I can't believe this, you're supposed to be ten years old."

Reeling from this attack, Max could only manage a feeble response. "Twelve years old," he said weakly.

"You think this is a game?" Nick bellowed.

Max knew that there was no excuse for what he had done, but he still wanted to try to explain what had happened. "Dad, I'm really sorry, I was coming to look for you —" he began.

Nick cut him off with a roar. "Why?" he asked sarcastically. "So we can have a day at the ballpark? Get a couple of rods and go *fishing*?"

No, they had never gone fishing. They had never gone to a baseball game. The simple truth was that in twelve years, they had never done *anything* together. "Dad, please," Max said quietly.

"I told you, I'm not your dad!" Nick shouted.

In front of them, a car horn blared. Nick wrenched the wheel over, just missing a skidding pickup. He had been so busy yelling at Max that he hadn't been paying attention to the road at all. They had come very close to being in a terrible accident.

"Look what you made me do!" he said furiously.

Max blinked as hard as he could, fighting to hold back tears. When Nick saw how upset Max was, his rage suddenly dissolved.

"Aw, gee," he said, and turned the car onto a deserted side street.

He pulled over to the curb and turned off the engine. They sat for a few minutes without speaking. Max slouched down in his seat, refusing to look at him.

Nick rolled down his window and took a deep breath of fresh air. Then he turned to his unhappy son, but no words came out. He reached out to touch his son's cheek, but Max flinched away from him. Nick sighed, and withdrew his hand. When he spoke, his voice was very soft.

"All these years," he mused. "Why'd you have to come *now*, Max?"

Max couldn't bring himself to answer right away. "Mom's going to marry Travis," he mumbled. "I thought I'd never see you again."

Nick shook his head. Max sensed that his father was finally beginning to understand how much Max needed him, and how much Max had looked up to him.

"I guess you must have thought I was really something," Nick said wryly.

Max shrugged, still refusing to meet his eyes. "I never knew what to think," he answered. "You were gone."

"Yeah." Nick ran his hands back through his hair and then rubbed his temples. "Well, now you know. . . ."

Yes, now Max knew, and he didn't like what he had discovered.

Nick took Max by the face and looked deep into his son's eyes. "Max," he said firmly. "You don't want to live my life. You have a choice. I don't. You understand?"

By now Max's face was streaked with tears and he wiped his sweatshirt sleeve across his eyes. No matter how hard he tried, he *didn't* understand.

Nick leaned closer. "Guys like me can't just walk away and pretend it didn't happen," he said regretfully. "Do you know how many cops would love to lock me up?"

Max looked up at his father, completely lost.

Nick didn't offer any explanation. "Look, I want to tell you something, Max," he said. "There are no second chances in life. No second chances. Remember that." Then he stared out the window at the cars and pedestrians passing by on the main street.

Max cleared his throat, so that his father would look over at him. When Nick did, Max held up the master tape.

Nick stared, obviously astonished that Max had had it with him the entire time.

Max set the tape silently on the dashboard and then opened his door. He got out of the car without a single word.

Nick gave him a rueful smile, as though there

was nothing left to say. So he just started the engine and drove away.

Max stood on the sidewalk and watched as his father got smaller and smaller. Finally, he couldn't see the car at all anymore.

His father had driven out of his life, and there was nothing that Max could do about it.

Over at the Music Boxx, Malik and his thugs were waiting for Nick to come back. They sat in his office, watching the video monitors. A surveillance tape that had been taken of the main recording studio earlier that day was playing on the screens. It showed Max and Kazaam searching the files for the master tape. Their voices were clearly audible and their faces were easy to recognize.

Malik watched in astonishment as the tape showed Kazaam slamming his hand down on the boom box. Electrical charges shot out, and sparks flew into the air.

Foad and Sam were also staring at this scene, looking astounded.

"Did you see that?!" Foad asked.

Hassem nodded. He was the one who had located the surveillance tape in the first place. "I told you," he said. "It's no ordinary boom box."

Hassem hit the remote control and fast-forwarded to the moment when the master tape suddenly spun into existence. The tape hovered magically above the boom box, supported by some unseen force.

Malik watched intently as Max snatched the tape out of the air. Then Kazaam and his "magical box" created another "time-phase change" and Max disappeared. Malik's greedy eyes brightened, and a sly smile came to his lips.

"It has *nothing* to do with the box," he decided. He knew that the magic had everything to do with — Kazaam!

Unaware of what they had just seen, Nick stepped into the room.

"If you're looking for this, I found it," he said. He held up the master tape for all of them to see.

Malik's hand snaked out and he swiftly shut off all of the monitors. He examined the recovered tape. Then he tossed it absentmindedly to Sam.

"Start production," he ordered. "I want the first run packed and shipped by sunrise."

Sam nodded, and hurried down to the recording studio with the tape.

Now that the tape had been returned, Nick started to leave the room.

Malik got up and pulled him back.

"Stick around, Nick," he said, with a smile that oozed greed. "I'd like to talk to you for a minute about . . . your son."

19

It was evening, and Max had gone to his trusty abandoned garage to think. He had been there for hours, staring straight ahead at nothing. A piece of Kazaam's magical bike lay among the other junk at the base of an immense stack of pickup truck beds.

Perched high above them, Max sat in his battered bucket seat. Through the open roof above, a night breeze ruffled his hair.

Suddenly, he jumped out of his chair. There *was* still a way to help his father, after all. All he had to do was find Kazaam!

Kazaam was just wrapping up his last number at the Music Boxx. The rocking, boisterous audience was enjoying every second of his performance.

"I'm a man of the ages, straight out of the pages, that paid Scheherazade's wages — hang on, I'm contagious!" Kazaam rapped happily. *"I'm outra-*

geous, spontaneous, can't contain this — I am KA-ZAAM!"

He finished with a burst of genie pyrotechnics, and the crowd roared its approval. Kazaam could only beam as he listened to all of the applause. Being a celebrity was the most fun he had ever had!

The stage manager was standing in the wings. He signaled for Kazaam to leave the stage, so that the show could go on. Kazaam took two more curtain calls, and then finally obeyed the signal.

Instantly, Kazaam was the center of attention. Someone wiped him down with a thick towel, a roadie pulled off his radio microphone, and Asia handed him a cool drink. Kazaam sipped some of the soda, feeling giddy with the rush of his success.

"Look at 'em, baby!" he gloated as he pointed at the still-cheering crowd. "There's over five hundred people out there, and they love me. Am I the bomb? Am I *doin'* it, or what?"

"You're doin' it," Asia said with a smile. "Oh, yes, you're definitely doin' it."

Kazaam frowned, trying to figure out what she meant by that.

Max came pushing through the crush of attendants. He grabbed Kazaam by his elaborate costume and dragged him off to the side.

"Kazaam, I want my last wish!" he said urgently.

Kazaam was so surprised that he started choking on his soda.

"Wait a minute. Say again?" Kazaam asked, once he had stopped coughing.

"My *third wish*," Max repeated.

Max could see the stage manager waving both arms at them. The chanting audience was begging for another encore, and the stage manager was trying to get his new star's attention. He was shouting something at Kazaam.

It was so loud backstage that Max could barely hear himself think. He stopped for a minute to collect himself. "I wish my dad had a second chance," he said.

Kazaam looked puzzled.

Seeing his uncertainty, Max quickly explained the situation. "You know, like a different life," he said. "Another chance."

Kazaam shook his head. He was so relieved that he could barely hide his feelings. Once he gave Max his third wish, Kazaam would have to go back into his boom box. "Sorry," he responded. "No can do, buddy."

"You have to, Kazaam," Max pleaded with him. "I need your help."

The stage manager was now waving a large white towel at them. "Klass K!" he yelled, using Kazaam's new stage name. "Hey, K! Over here!"

Kazaam was concentrating so hard on Max's problem that he didn't even notice the stage manager. "Kid, we've been over this," he said patiently. "New lives, destiny? Kazaam can't do the ethereal."

Out of the corner of his eye, Max noticed Asia watching them from across the room.

"Kazaam, I need this more than anything I've ever needed in my life," Max said in complete frustration. "Can't you even try?!"

Kazaam sighed and shook his head. "Believe me, I have. For thousands of —"

"Try harder!" Max begged him. "Please!"

In spite of himself, Kazaam was starting to lose his temper. How many times did he have to explain his genie limitations?

"Maybe you're not listening," he said stiffly. "I *cannot* do it!"

Max could feel tears forming in his eyes again. "Kazaam, I *gotta* make a wish!"

The stage manager came over, looking impatient. "Hey, K," he said. "You going on, or what?"

Caught between the stage manager and the corner that Max was backing him into, Kazaam flared up.

"Haven't you learned, yet?" he asked Max. "Life ain't about dreams and wishes. It's about what you got, and what you can do with it!"

A roadie came over and pinned a new microphone on Kazaam's vest.

"Please, Kazaam," Max said, feeling both frantic and guilty. "You don't understand. My dad's in trouble, and — it's all my fault."

Kazaam let out an exhausted breath. Too many people had been asking him for too many things, for too many years. "I can't just snap my fingers and make you all happy!" he said. "I'm not some Djinn. I am what I am. Period. End of story. Okay?"

All Max could hear was Kazaam's refusal, and he felt betrayed.

"You just don't want to grant the third wish, do you?" he asked, his voice dripping bitterness. "You've got all this and now you don't want to go back into your box. You said you were my friend!"

Kazaam lashed back, his own voice stinging. "Friend?" he repeated incredulously. "*Friend*? Don't you remember? I'm just your *genie*."

They stared at each other, both out of breath and at a loss for words.

"What you are is *nothing*," Max said.

The tears in his eyes spilled over, and he ran away. Kazaam had been the one person he thought he could trust. Now it seemed as though he couldn't trust *anyone*.

Max kept running, until he slammed right into Asia's outstretched arms.

"Max," she said, looking concerned. "What is it?"

"Nothing," he said sulkily, and tried to twist away from her.

She held on more tightly. "Max, come on. You can tell me."

119

Max glared up at her with furious eyes. "Just get out of my way!" he said. "I got something to do!"

He jerked free and rushed into the crowd. Asia went after him, but Max quickly lost her in the swelling throng.

On the dance floor, the crowd chanted Kazaam's name over and over. The band members looked into the wings for their leader. Kazaam was trying to calm down and focus on his next rap before he took the stage. The scene with Max had left him feeling extremely rattled.

Asia threaded her way through the people backstage until she had reached Kazaam's side.

"What's going on with Max?" she asked, her expression very troubled.

Unsure how much of the truth he could tell her, Kazaam hesitated. "Nothing, baby," he said finally. "No big deal. It's just a phase."

Asia shook her head. "I don't think so. Kazaam, he's really upset —"

Kazaam cut her off before she could get any further. "What kid isn't?" he asked in a cold, flat voice. "Hey, wish me luck, will ya? I have to do my big encore."

"I didn't realize how fast the poison worked," she said disdainfully.

Kazaam bit his lip, not sure why she was so mad at him. "What do you mean?"

"You've changed," Asia said. "All you care about is yourself now."

"That's not true," Kazaam protested. "I just — they want an encore, that's all."

"I'm just glad I found out now what you're really like," Asia said. "Before I started caring about you even more than I already do."

"Come on, K!" the stage manager yelled over to them. "Let's move!"

Kazaam looked out at the stage, and then back at Asia. He didn't know what to do.

"Good-bye, Kazaam, it was nice knowing you," Asia said, and then she walked away.

"Asia, come back!" he called after her.

But she was gone.

20

Kazaam stood alone for a second, trying to recover himself. His two favorite people, Max and Asia, both hated him now. How had everything gone from being so great, to being so awful, in the space of five minutes?

Just then, Malik swaggered out of the crowd and gave Kazaam a big bear hug.

"Look what you have!" he proclaimed. Then he kissed Kazaam on both cheeks in a very phony, showbiz way. "Do you know how jealous you're making me?"

Kazaam waved that aside, dismissing the compliment. "Hey, I'm just tellin' my story," he said weakly.

"No!" Malik assured him. "It's much more. You're a sensation!"

"Klass K! Klass K! Klass K!" the crowd chanted as they waited for him to come back out.

Kazaam realized that somehow, the noises of applause and people chanting his name didn't sound as nice as they had a few minutes ago.

Malik grabbed him by the shoulders, staring up into his eyes. "You have a — you are —" He stopped, struggling to find the right words to praise him. Then he whispered an Arabic saying Kazaam had not heard in many years.

"'A sultan's gold?'" Kazaam asked, translating the phrase.

Malik was delighted. "Oh, you speak!" he said, seeming surprised. "Very good!"

Kazaam shrugged, afraid that he had revealed too much. "Well, uh —" he started.

"Have faith in yourself! You *are* the sultan's gold!" Malik told him.

His spirits buoyed, Kazaam began to nod. He reached down for his boom box, but it was gone.

"Hey, my box!" he cried.

"No, no, don't worry about the little things," Malik said, and pointed him toward the stage. "Listen. Your public calls."

Kazaam listened cooperatively, but he still wasn't sure if this was a call he wanted to answer.

"Trust me," Malik said smoothly. "This is my world. And right now, you're the biggest part of it."

Uneasily, Kazaam shifted his weight from one big high-top to the other. Was this what he really wanted?

Malik lifted a hand to signal Kazaam's entourage. They surrounded Kazaam, toweling him down and primping and powdering him. He was getting the full star treatment!

Carried by Malik's enthusiasm, Kazaam faced the stage. Out there, his public was waiting for him. He took a deep breath and stepped onto the stage. When the crowd saw him, they burst into applause.

"Rock my world, Klass K!" the stage manager shouted.

Kazaam nodded — and started to perform for his fans.

Malik faded back into the shadows. His greedy eyes never left Kazaam, his new meal ticket. As far as he was concerned, he had accomplished his selfish mission.

"My sultan's gold lives in a genie's lamp," he crooned to himself. "Mine, all mine."

Max raced toward Nick's office and flung the door open. There was a very tense meeting going on. Nick was surrounded by El Baz, Foad, and Hassem. When he saw Hassem and the other goons, he gasped.

"Get *out* of here!" Nick ordered him. "Right now!"

After a moment of uncertainty, Max started to run. He slammed right into Kazaam's boom box. He smiled, feeling relieved that his friend had come to help him, after all. Then, to his horror, he saw that Malik was the one holding the boom box, not Kazaam.

Foad moved to shut the door. Now Max was trapped in the room with these evil thieves!

"At long last," Malik said with a sneer. "Your father's been very modest about your accomplishments, Max." He held out the boom box. "Look familiar?"

Max stared at the boom box. How had Malik gotten it away from Kazaam? Was Kazaam okay?

"That's right," Malik said smugly. "*I've* got the box now, and *you're* on your last wish."

Max glanced at his father, but Nick obviously had no idea what Malik was talking about.

Nick strode over to join them. "Malik, let's stop the little games," he suggested. "I don't know what you're talking about, and neither does he."

Malik kept talking to Max as though Nick hadn't said a word. "Now, son, you can't keep all these secrets from *me*," he said, holding the boom box just out of reach. "You're going to do exactly what I tell you to do."

Nick tried to get in between them. "Come on, you've got the tape, Malik. Leave him alone," he argued. "He's just a boy."

Faster than Nick could react, Malik snatched a heavy paperweight from the desk. Then he slammed it viciously across the side of Nick's head.

Nick groaned and staggered into the wall. Then his eyes closed and he slumped to the floor.

Malik turned back to Max. "I think you'd better make the wish," he advised. "I get the genie, and everything my heart desires. And if you try anything clever, dearly beloved Nick will . . . wake up dead."

El Baz lifted the unconscious Nick off the floor. He pulled out a knife and held it under Nick's chin.

Max's face went pale. He knew that he couldn't make that wish, and even if he did, Kazaam wouldn't grant it. But he couldn't sacrifice his father, either. His only choice was to start talking, and start talking *fast*.

"I don't want to pop your bubble or anything," he said to Malik. "But the truth is, this genie stinks."

Malik looked startled. "What do you mean?" he asked, holding the boom box protectively.

"He's not normal," Max said simply. "Most wishes, he can't even do. Then there's all these rules. And even if you find a wish, he's gotta clear it with this review board or something, and there's a forty-eight hour turnaround, and when it finally comes back —"

Out of patience, Malik held up his hand for silence. "Your third wish will be, quote, 'I want Malik to have all the money in the world,'" he ordered. "Now, do it!"

Max shrugged a no-can-do shrug. "But, see? I

already wished for that!" he answered. "And the board said, if you do that, everyone else goes broke, and money's not worth anything anymore."

Malik shoved him roughly against the wall. He moved closer until his breath was hot in Max's face. "Then I'll take all the money and give some of it back," he hissed. "Make my wish now!"

"I-I can't," Max insisted, trying to think of a way out. "It's not like you can just shout — HEY KAZAAM, I NEED YOU RIGHT NOW! — and suddenly you're in front of him. You can't just say, KAZAAM, HELP!"

Malik must have realized that Max was trying to call for help. So he quickly wrapped his hands around Max's neck, choking off any further cries.

Max gulped, and closed his eyes. He just hoped that Kazaam had been able to hear him!

21

Down on the dance floor, Kazaam was rocking and rolling, and hipping and hopping. Surrounded by the throb of the music and the roar of the fans, he felt the strange twitch in his ear again.

But the band jammed on, and the crowd kept cheering. The twitch must have been his imagination. Kazaam shook his head, and went back to jamming along with them.

Upstairs, Malik kept ranting and raving. He had all sorts of plans for what he was going to do, once he was given all of the money in the world.

"After you make me the wealthiest man in the world, it'll be my turn," he said, his eyes crazed with ambition. "I'll wish myself into the most powerful man, then into the most admired man, and when I'm stuffed with fame and fortune, my *third* wish will be —"

In one furious move, Nick vaulted from the floor. He elbowed El Baz in the neck. Then he grabbed a

computer monitor off his desk and banged it
against Foad's head. Now it was time to take on
Malik!

"Get out the door!" he yelled to Max.

Max scurried out into the hallway. He looked
over his shoulder for Nick, but his father wasn't
there. He hesitated, and started back toward the
office.

Nick raced out the door and grabbed him.

"Come on!" he said. "Over here!"

They dashed down the hall, with the thugs only
seconds behind them.

Unaware of the desperate struggle upstairs,
Kazaam was still performing. He dove into his
final number, full of energy and enthusiasm.

"Trapped in a box, like a premature burial," he
rapped. But then he lost his place and had to stop
for a minute.

The band kept playing, and urging him on.

Kazaam thought some more, and then got back
on track. *"Used to be down, used to be funereal,
used to be mull, in a space cemeterial!"* he rapped.

For a second there, he'd thought he'd felt another twitch in his ear. . . .

Nick and Max tore down the upstairs hallway.
Sam was standing just ahead of them. His hand
slipped under his coat for his gun, and he rushed in
their direction.

Nick and Max spun away from him and began retracing their steps.

"I know a better way," Nick yelled. "Follow me!"

They flew around the corner to a locked door. It was a keypad lock, and Nick punched in the combination. The steel bolt slid back and the door swung open.

"This way!" Nick said, and dragged Max into a dark tunnel.

With Kazaam's music throbbing underfoot, Nick and Max raced through the echoing tunnel. Sam, now joined by Foad and El Baz, chased after them.

Nick and Max fled out of the tunnel into a large workroom. Max faltered, unnerved by what he saw. They were in a secret warehouse facility. It was the nerve center of Malik's illegal operations.

Crates were stacked everywhere, and workers were lined up behind long tables. The workers were packing counterfeit CDs into empty guitar amplifiers. Then they would reassemble the amplifiers. It was a clever way to smuggle the bootlegged CDs out of the building without anyone noticing.

"Come on!" Nick said, and he pulled Max through the maze of stacked boxes ready for shipment.

Sam and the others were getting closer every second!

Downstairs on the dance floor, Kazaam was still plunging through his newest hip-hop tale.

"But I peeled that spiel, got real with a new meal," he rapped. *"Now I'm sucking down life, like a cutlet of veal!"*

The audience rocked along with him, almost bringing the house down with their cheers. Kazaam felt as if they wanted him to be the headline act every night!

And, so far, he hadn't felt that twitch again.

Nick and Max charged up a staircase to the manufacturing floor. Nick guided Max through a small opening and into a large chamber. Max was dumbfounded by the size of this hidden factory.

In the center of the floor, a steel-mesh cage surrounded the humming machinery of the counterfeiting operation. Various workers tended stamping machines, laser etchers, and screening presses. Max wasn't sure what all of those machines did, but they certainly looked complicated.

Since the workers obviously recognized Nick, they moved out of his way. But when they saw Max, they looked confused. Only authorized personnel were allowed to be on the floor. Max was a stranger — and a very young one, at that.

Sam ran into the chamber with Hassem and Foad. They were all perspiring and out of breath.

"Stop them!" Sam bellowed as he pointed at the fleeing Nick and Max. "Don't let them get away!"

Nick pushed Max behind the hulking machines, where he would be safe.

"No, keep those men right where they are!" Nick ordered the workers. "They're traitors!"

The confused workers didn't know who to believe. So they tried to obey all of the orders. Chaos broke out all over the room as everyone starting yelling at once.

Max huddled behind the biggest machine, more scared than he could ever remember.

"Kazaam," he whispered. "Where are you, Kazaam? Help me!"

Outside the Music Boxx, Max's mother Alice was trying to get past the bouncers. They must have felt her outfit was too casual, so they had refused to let her go in. But Alice wasn't about to take no for an answer!

"I've got a boy in there, and he's in trouble," she told them desperately. "So you grow a spine and help me, or I'm going to shove your 'rules' down your throat!"

The blond bouncer shrugged. "Sorry, lady. Rules are rules."

"We got a dress code here," his partner explained.

Alice was in no mood to hear any excuses. So she ducked underneath their arms and ran into the club as they yelled in protest.

She could feel in her heart that her son was in big trouble!

*   *   *

Kazaam was still strutting back and forth on the stage.

"When I handle the fans, I'll be magisterial," he promised. *"With my new friends, I'm already imperial. One snap of my fingers, got a scoop of Ben and Jerrial. Be living so rich, better watch my arterials!"*

The crowd laughed and clapped and begged for more.

Kazaam smiled, but he was really just going through the motions. He searched the crowd for a single familiar face, but they were all strangers.

Suddenly, even though he was the center of attention, he felt very lonely. . . . But he thrust aside the increasingly uncomfortable sensation he was feeling. He raised his arms for his finale.

"So don't get me down," he rapped. *"With those old thoughts ethereal!"* He held the last note for a long time, to heighten the effect.

Once again, the crowd screamed for more!

Sam, Hassem, and Foad separated and began searching the manufacturing floor. Nick and Max edged around the counterfeiting cage, trying to avoid them. Max was hiding behind a stamping machine, as it pounded out endless bootlegs of the previous night's concert.

There was a hoarse shout, and El Baz leaped toward them. Nick rose up to meet him in midair. Max was terrified — his father was endangering himself. He wanted to buy Max some time. Nick was trying to protect him.

"Max!" he shouted as he struggled with El Baz. "There's another staircase over there. Run!"

Driven by his father's voice, Max raced away from the fight. He dodged around a thick pillar, trying to escape.

"No, Max!" Nick shouted after him. "Not through —"

Before he could finish his sentence, Foad wrestled him down to the floor and clapped his hand over his mouth.

"Lock him up," Hassem said fiercely to two of the workers. "The rest of you, come on! Get that kid!"

Max kept running until he found himself heading straight for an empty elevator shaft. His eyes widened as he saw the terrible danger he was in. He slid to a stop, his toes teetering at the lip of an abyss.

At the last second, he managed to recover his balance. He turned to go the other way — and stopped cold.

Malik was standing in front of him, wearing one of his evil smiles.

Max was trapped!

22

Max knew that this was a life or death situation. He tried one final bluff.

"I'm the one with the wish, I'm the one with the power," he said, as his teeth chattered with fear. "Kazaam is my genie, and as long as I'm standing here, he's going to do what I tell him! And *you* guys are going nowhere."

Malik just smiled.

Suddenly Max realized that all he had done was make one thing blindingly clear.

"Then I guess my only problem," Malik said gleefully, "is that you're still standing."

He reached forward and deliberately gave Max a push. Max reeled on the edge, with his hands clawing the air. Then he fell right into the elevator shaft!

Downstairs, Kazaam was finishing his rap.

"*I know who I am,*" he said. "*I'm —*" Suddenly, the words seemed to stick in his throat. "*I'm —*"

"*Mr. Material!*" the audience shouted in unison.

135

Kazaam whirled around as though he had been physically struck. He staggered dizzily across the stage. Reeling from the force of the feeling, he straightened up. He wasn't sure what had just happened, but he felt very strange.

Down on the dance floor, Alice was pointing at him. Even though she was shouting, her voice could barely be heard in the commotion.

"Mr. Lamb!" she yelled.

In that instant, all of Kazaam's doubts and fears came together and he knew what had happened. Without another thought, he vanished!

The audience gasped. In the abrupt silence, the only sound was Kazaam's microphone clattering to the floor. Then the crowd erupted with joy.

It was the best performance they had ever seen!

Kazaam rematerialized up on the manufacturing floor. He found himself standing in front of his boom box. Malik was holding it, and chuckling insanely.

The boom box jolted and jumped as though it were alive.

"All right," Malik breathed. "It works!" He waved Kazaam forward with one hand. "Now be a good genie. Get in the box."

"I don't understand," Kazaam said slowly.

"You've been *called*," Malik answered, and held the boom box out.

The cassette door was open and there was a soft

hissing and a whirling wind. The wind drew Kazaam forward, but then he recovered himself.

"Where's Max?" he asked, his fears rising.

Malik just smiled. "Max has terminated your contract," he said. "You have a new master." He shook the boom box temptingly. "Now, hup-hup! Get in."

Kazaam knew what that must mean, but he didn't want to believe it. Max was fine. He *had* to be. "But — I haven't granted the last wish yet," Kazaam protested.

"Trust me," Malik said with a wide grin. "He won't be asking for any more."

Kazaam's heart jumped into his throat. "What did you do to him?!" he screamed.

Furious, Kazaam tried to collar him, but his hand went right through Malik. They both stared at Kazaam's arm, buried deep in Malik's chest. Kazaam frowned, and pulled his hand out.

"It's begun. . . . " Malik chuckled.

Shocked, Kazaam stared at his own shoe, as it started to disappear. The wind from the boom box had entwined around Kazaam's feet. Now it was stealing them away, molecule by molecule.

"No!" Kazaam said helplessly.

Malik looked triumphant. "Yes!" he shouted.

Kazaam put a hand out to steady himself, but now his hand had also thinned into smoke. He went down onto his knees, struggling as hard as he could against the call of the boom box.

"Not all there, Klass K?" Foad chortled.

Malik and his goons burst into laughter.

Kazaam focused his will with every ounce of strength and his fists solidified. He grabbed Foad and El Baz, and lifted them right off the floor. He hurled them into the counterfeiting cage, and they crashed onto the delicate machines inside.

The machines started to short out and give off sparks. Flames exploded through the dry ceiling timbers in a welter of thick, oily smoke.

Sam and Hassem exchanged worried glances. But Kazaam just charged toward Malik.

"Hold him back!" Malik told his henchmen. "This won't take long!"

Sam sprang onto Kazaam's back and tried to throttle him. Kazaam threw him off and head-butted him across the room. Hassem tried to tackle him by hitting his knees, but Kazaam just punted him through the ceiling.

Now Malik was the only one still standing.

"You can't hurt me!" he said with an insane light in his eyes. "I'm your Master!"

Kazaam looked at him, his expression cold and determined. "I'm *never* going to be your slave," he said.

He lunged forward and plucked the boom box away from Malik. Then he hoisted Malik over his head.

"Where's Max?!" he shouted.

"He-he — fell down the shaft," Malik stammered,

his eyes bulging with fear. "There was nothing I could do! Please don't hurt me!"

"Wish not granted," Kazaam answered.

He wadded Malik into a ball of shrieking panic and pounded him into the floor. Malik began bouncing into the air and Kazaam slam-dunked him into a trash chute.

Now, it was time to find Max!

Outside, the last of the nightclubbers were fleeing from the building. The fire was spreading, and the whole building was starting to burn. Alice was watching the disaster with tears rolling down her cheeks.

At that moment, a fire engine rolled up. It was Travis and the other firefighters from his station house.

"I think Max is in there!" Alice shouted.

Oily smoke rolled out of the building. Then a cloud of flame erupted through the windows. Alice lurched forward, ready to rescue her son by herself.

"Trust me," Travis said, and he grabbed an ax from the fire truck. "I'll save him!" he promised, and then he charged into the burning building.

Alice closed her eyes. Now both of the people she cared about most were in danger!

Kazaam jumped into the elevator shaft, landing lightly at the bottom. The boom box wind was still stealing molecules from him, but Kazaam ignored that. He had more important things to worry about now. Max was lying very still at the base of the shaft, and Kazaam lifted him into his arms.

"Hey, tough guy," he said gently.

There was no answer. Max had not survived the fall. . . .

23

Kazaam carried Max's lifeless body to the now-evacuated dance floor. He stood on the deserted stage, struggling against the reality that, for the one time it counted, he was helpless. He stopped and screamed his anguish to the heavens.

"No!" he shouted, and then looked down at Max's pale face. "In five thousand years, you're the only friend I've ever had," he said softly, tears filling his eyes. "And when you needed my help, I didn't even try. If I had to spend another five thousand years in a lamp, a compass — even a boom box! — I wouldn't care. I just wish I could have granted your wish."

As he spoke, a glow started to emanate from his chest.

"I wish I could have filled your heart," Kazaam went on.

The glow became white, and then blue. It flowed

into Max's chest, and then started to envelop them both.

"Max, you are the sultan's gold," Kazaam whispered. "And I . . . I am only Kazaam."

The light grew until Max and Kazaam were incandescent. It gave off a brilliant radiance, and a warm glow slowly enfolded them. Kazaam kept his eyes tightly shut as he prayed. He would give anything to have his friend back.

But then, suddenly, Max's eyes *opened.*

"Do you have to shine that in my eyes?" he asked, squinting in the brightness.

Kazaam opened his eyes, astonished. In this moment of wonder and joy, he didn't notice that the boom box wind had reversed, and was now flowing *into* him.

"Max! Y-you're alive!" he gasped.

Max grinned at him. "Will you please put me down already?" he asked.

Kazaam set him gently on the floor. "I don't get it," he said. "*I* made a wish — and I granted it?"

Then, with a flash, his body began to change. From the waist down, he was a mass of churning ions and splitting atoms.

"Kazaam, what's happening?!" Max shouted.

"I-I don't know," Kazaam said, terrified in spite of himself. "This — it's never been like this before."

"You can't leave me," Max said. "I haven't asked for my third wish."

"But, you did," Kazaam reminded him. "You asked for a second chance for your father." He held up his hand when Max started to protest. "It was a wish from your heart. It's a *perfect* wish. And it's done."

Just then, Kazaam was hit with a second flash. For one instant, his whole being was converted to pure energy.

"What was that?" Max asked uneasily.

"I don't know," Kazaam said, looking down at himself. "I feel . . . I feel. . . . " Then an ebullient grin spread across his face. "Free!"

A final flash hit like a thunderclap. Then Kazaam was transformed into an immense, glowing face.

"You — you're —" Max was so awed he couldn't speak. "Wow."

For the first time, Kazaam understood what had happened.

"I'm Djinn," he said, also sounding awed. "And I'm free."

"No, please," Max begged him. "Don't go, Kazaam!"

Kazaam's ghostly face floated closer. "You don't need me anymore," he said softly. "You have the magic in your heart, Max. In our hearts, we're all Djinn, and we're all free."

Max nodded, trying not to cry.

"Max, what I want is for you to have your wish," Kazaam said. "Now, ask me . . . *anything*."

Neither of them noticed a tentacle of smoke seeping from the boom box's open mouth. It spiraled down the staircase and into the club.

Max looked up at his genie. "I don't know," he said. "There's so much — I mean, you, and Travis, my mom, Dad —" He stopped. "I just wish everyone could be okay."

"I like okay," Kazaam said with deep satisfaction. "Okay is good." He loomed closer. "You don't need me anymore, Max. You have the magic, in *your* heart. That's the true power."

The smoke tentacle slithered across the stage, moving closer and closer to Kazaam.

"Don't you see, Max," Kazaam explained in his gigantic whisper. "I'm Djinn." He closed his eyes for a second. "And I am — Kazaam." When he opened his eyes, he smiled.

"That's it?" Max asked. "You granted the wish?"

Kazaam smiled kindly at him. "Like the main man did, with the loaves and the fish," he answered.

Behind him, the boom box's whirling vortex suddenly reared up with a terrible sucking hiss. Kazaam's face began to vibrate, and light burst out from inside him. It grew and grew into a huge, radiant sun.

"The power . . . is in your heart," Kazaam's voice said from somewhere inside the light.

With that last piece of advice ringing in his ears, Max found himself being lifted into the air. His body streamed like a comet over a barrier of burning debris. He didn't know what was happening, but he was sure that he was going to die!

24

Max screamed as he flew through the air. All he could see was the building starting to crumble and a flaming roof falling toward him. At the last second, Travis caught him only feet from a wall of billowing fire. Max stared at him in a daze.

Travis grinned at him. "I make a catch like that, and you don't even say 'nice save'?" he asked.

Then Travis turned to face the curtain of flames. Sheltering Max's head against his chest, he charged through the inferno. He carried Max outside and set him down in the middle of the street. They both sucked in lungfuls of cold night air.

Alice rushed over to them. "Oh, thank goodness!" she said. "You're both safe!"

Travis nodded, and ran back to help his fellow firefighters. The building was a total loss, but he could still help make sure that no one got hurt fighting the blaze.

Alice held Max, who was shivering. "I'll get you

a blanket," she said, and ran toward the nearest ambulance.

Staring into the swirling flames, Max saw a silhouetted figure. The figure staggered, coughed, and fell to its knees. It was Nick, alive and unburnt. Somehow, he had survived.

"I-I don't know what happened," he said between choking gasps. "All of a sudden, I was free...."

A faint smile crossed Max's lips.

"Your friend was there," Nick told him. "Said something about a second chance."

Max's smile widened.

Alice had returned with a blanket, which she placed around Max's shoulders.

Nick came over and knelt down in front of Max. "You're a good boy, Max," he said. "You've got a good heart. I've got a few things I let slide, a few people I owe. But after that, I want to come back and see you." He looked at Max shyly. "Maybe get a couple of rods, go fishing?"

Max looked at his father, man to man. "Sounds like a plan," he said.

Nick stood up. "If that's all right with you," he said to Alice.

Alice glanced at Travis, who had just come over to join her. Then she turned back to Nick and nodded.

Max looked from Nick, to Alice, to Travis, and knew that his wish *had* been granted. Everyone was going to be okay.

"Thanks," Nick said to Max, and patted him gently on the shoulder. "I'll see you soon, son."

Max nodded, and his father walked off into the darkness.

Travis bent down next to him. "Kind of a rough few days. You okay with all of this?" he asked.

Max, watching his father leave, nodded. "Yeah," he said. "I am."

"You sure?" Travis asked.

Max nodded again.

Travis backed away as Alice moved in closer. She hugged Max, and he hugged back tightly.

"Mom, can we go home?" he asked.

Alice smiled at him. "Sure," she said. "Come on."

They started to walk away, but then Max paused to look back at Travis.

"Hey!" he said cheerfully. "You coming, or what?"

Travis laughed. "You talking to *me*?" he responded in the same sort of tough-guy voice.

Max looked at his mother. "You sure you want to marry this guy?"

"That's the plan," Alice said.

Travis messed up Max's hair as the three of them started to walk down the street together.

"Look, I just want you to know," Max said to him. "I've been dealing with this woman for twelve straight years. You're looking at three baths a week. Trash detail. Cleaning your room."

Travis pretended to wince. "*Three* baths a week?" he asked. "Are you serious?"

"With *soap*," Alice said.

Travis winced harder, and shook his head. "I'm sorry. That's cold."

"Speaking of which," Max said brightly. "I could sure do with a cup of hot chocolate."

Just as he finished saying that, he stopped walking. Right smack in the middle of the street, a steaming cup of hot chocolate, piled high with whipped cream, had appeared.

Max picked up the cup, and then eyed the crowd. He squinted through the smoke until he finally located two familiar figures walking down the street.

One of them was a huge man wearing street clothes, and the other was Asia Moon.

"You don't get it," Kazaam was saying. "I'm *free*."

"Free to do what?" Asia asked.

Kazaam shrugged expansively. "Lady, I got plans," he said.

"The only plans *you* have are to grow old with me," Asia told him.

Kazaam laughed, loving the idea. "Yeah, well, don't blink, I'll disappear," he joked.

"No, you're in the real world now," she said. "And I'll tell you something else. You're going to get a job."

Kazaam stared at her. "A *job*?" he asked, sounding horrified.

"A *job*," she said firmly.

Seeing Kazaam's total dismay, Max couldn't help laughing. That was one Djinn who was *way* out of his league. Then he ran to catch up with his mother and Travis.

Everything really *was* going to be okay!